1-900-DEAD

Also by Tony Fennelly:

The Glory Hole Murders
The Closet Hanging
Kiss Yourself Goodbye
The Hippie in the Wall

1-900-DEAD

Tony Fennelly

St. Martin's Press
New York

Design by Nancy Resnick

Library of Congress Cataloging-in-Publication Data

Fennelly, Tony.
    1-900-dead / by Tony Fennelly.—1st ed.
      p.   cm.
    ISBN 0-312-14267-6
    I. Title.   II. Title: One-nine hundred dead.
   PS3556.E49A614   1997
   813'.54—DC20   96-5199
                             CIP

First Edition: January 1997

10 9 8 7 6 5 4 3 2 1

Dedicated to Richard Catoire

(The "One Night Stand" that failed.)

Acknowledgements

I wish to thank Patrick and Daniel O'Flaherty, the charming troubadours from Connemara who supplied me with the Gaelic.

Thanks also to Ken Reynolds, the "sees-all, knows-all" guru of Bywater.

1-900-DEAD

PROLOGUE

"*I*f she'd *really* been psychic, she'd've seen it coming."

"You'd think, huh?"

Apparently not, though. As Lt. Frank Washington noted, the famous "Mystic Delphine" looked as surprised as anybody at the sword protruding from her chest. But she wasn't actually seeing anything anymore, either in this world or in the one beyond it to which she had laid claim in countless TV ads.

"Hey, Frank!"

Officer Duffy stood in the center of the blood-splashed bedroom and pointed to an extravagant full-color poster on the south wall, then down again. "It's the same sword she swung around in her commercials."

He read the poster's caption aloud in a deep-voiced imitation of a television announcer: "LET THE QUEEN OF SWORDS, THE MYSTIC DELPHINE, UNLOCK THE SECRETS OF THE TAROT FOR YOU! Feature that."

"I'd say she tried to name her murderer." Washington squatted behind the stiffened remains. "According to the blood pattern, the victim must have been stabbed over there by the bed. Then she was able to crawl this far to the wall and write a capital *P.* It looks like she attempted a second letter but collapsed before she could finish it."

1

"In that case, she had to know the perp's name. So it wasn't your traditional New Orleans break-in-robbery-murder."

"Was this woman married?"

"No such luck. She was a spinster, and she lived alone."

"That's too bad." Washington straightened up with a groan. "Now we've got a case to solve."

I'm picking a card."

I spread the Medieval Tarot deck across the coffee table.

"This one is supposed to be for my future."

Julian, like all prosaic-minded husbands, rolled his eyes as I ran my hand over the cards till my ring finger tingled on one. I held that card up to him.

"The Magician," he said, not even trying to sound interested. "So, Margo, what is that supposed to mean?"

It was mid-November, and the space heater had made our living room too warm. I fanned myself with the card.

"I don't know. I'm not psychic."

"Your 'New Agers' persist in claiming that *everyone* has psychic ability."

"But there's always an asterisk next to that 'everyone' which leads down the page to a footnote stating: 'That is, of course, everyone *except* Margo Fortier of New Orleans.' "

"You've never even had a premonition?"

"Not so much as a cheap déjà vu experience."

I turned the card and studied "Number One" of the Major Arcana, the powerful Magician.

"Maybe I'm going to have an affair with Penn or Teller."

"I wouldn't think that likely."

"You're right." I reshuffled the deck. "I'm like that old Bruce Brown movie about looking for the perfect wave, except that with me it's a never-ending search for the perfect love affair."

"The poor misguided wretch would have to poke through some cobwebs."

"Yes, it has been a while."

Julian leaned back and crossed his impeccable ankles on the ottoman. "I, myself, have been forced to live like a monk these days. My social life has been limited to attending memorial services."

"What are you complaining about, Neg? You've got at least one a week down in the Quarter."

"Insensitive bitch."

We do more bickering than the Knesset, but actually, we get along quite well for two people who have nothing in common—except that we both like guys.

Julian is a New Orleans aristocrat, and I'm a bar girl from New Jersey. I'm ambitious, and he's not. Never had to be.

I get more dollar value out of the Fortier name than he ever thought of doing. In fact, I've been a professional "Mrs. Fortier" for all of the eighteen years since we took the vows. His uptight, class-obsessed family couldn't exactly approve of an ex-stripper for a daughter-in-law. But the whole crowd of snobs was so tickled that he was even marrying a genetic female, they could hardly be choosy about pedigree.

He had turned his attention back to the TV which showed "A Current Affair" for today, Sunday, Nov. 14th 1993.

Now a commercial was on in which soigneé Liz Ashley was bragging about the slimming properties of a liquid diet drink and purring that it came in candy form too.

"Look!" I shook a finger at the screen. "Notice how when she starts pulling that candy bar out of the wrapper, the camera cuts away before she gets it all the way out. They don't want us to know how puny the thing actually is."

"Are you considering Slim-Fast? Have you become dissatisfied with your physical envelope?"

4

"What do you think about a hundred and forty-five pounds, naked before breakfast?"

"I think I don't want to witness the weigh-in."

"That's ten pounds too much," I hoisted my bust. "But I was flat-chested all my life, and now I've these great bosoms, see? And if I lose weight, they'll be the first to go."

"So?"

"So, this is the preeminent question: Should I go on a diet or just buy a girdle?"

He nodded carefully. "Before you decide, you might envision the look of horror and betrayal on the face of a potential lover once you squirm *out* of the postulated girdle and your cellulite starts rippling in the breeze of the ceiling fan."

"If he's a breast man, maybe he wouldn't notice."

"But if he *is* a breast man"—Julian wrinkled his classic nose—"wouldn't he sort of, well, prefer *firm* ones? I mean, I don't know anything about it, but—"

"No! He'd like them nice and squishy, like mine."

"If you say so. You can always resort to liposuction. It banishes the fat cells for life."

"But I'm afraid to amputate a natural part of my anatomy. What if someday I need those fat cells for sustenance?"

"Are you afraid of a worldwide famine?"

"That's not likely. But everyone dies of something. Mine may be cancer or some other disease that reduces me to skin and bones. The more I start with, the longer I'll have to live. Right?"

"I see what you mean. It would take a good year for you to waste away at your present bulk."

" 'Healthy mind in healthy body,' " I averred. "I've been using the principles of *feng shui,* inviting positive energy into my life by changing my environment."

He blinked slowly. "How is that supposed to work?"

"I want to attract a lover, right? So I bought red sheets for my bed, and I've been burning red candles and incense every night."

"It sounds like you're trying to attract Ferdinand the Bull."

"At least he'd have the necessary stamina."

"My word!" Julian clapped his hands to his virgin ears. "Your vulgarity is epic!" Then the hands went down. "However, I am imbued with a Christlike level of tolerance. And in keeping with that, I've brought you something that should actually advance your wanton agenda."

He reached into his Chippendale magazine rack and pulled out a slim volume bound in dove gray and adorned with embossed ivory lace and pink roses. I accepted the book and held it at arm's length to read the title.

"*Miss Georgia's Guide to the Secrets of Charm.* Huh? Why on Earth would I read this?"

"Because as Havelock Ellis said, 'It is indispensable to women.' " Julian sat back in his recliner. " 'Charm is a woman's strength, just as strength is a man's charm.' "

"So?"

"So, as Miss Georgia herself says right there on page two . . . " He pointed. "That indispensable attribute 'is a skill that can be learned like any other.' "

"You mean to sit there and claim that I need some book to tell me how to behave?"

"Desperately."

"Criminy! I'm always tripping all over myself to be charming to people."

Julian shook his head. "Margo, your idea of charm is to go up to a fat, bald guy and say, 'Hi! I like fat, bald guys.' "

"But I do. Why shouldn't he be flattered?"

"Maybe the poor soul would rather you didn't even notice that he's fat and bald."

"Didn't notice?" I snapped the volume shut. "I don't want the man to think I'm dense. Then he wouldn't respect me."

"My dear girl, you have been reading respect into a posture that is actually no less than white-faced, toe-curling apprehension."

"All right, so I'll read your stupid book." I flopped backward onto the couch, being past the age where I take the trouble to lower myself with style and grace when there's no audience present. "But it will be a puredee waste of time."

"Speaking of which, what time is it?" Julian grabbed the remote, as husbands will, and started channel surfing. "They're supposed to be running a Lee Harvey Oswald special."

"Another one? But we already saw the Marina Oswald movie, the young Jack documentary, the Jackie retrospective, and two assassination reenactments."

"It's the thirtieth anniversary. We'll see a lot more on the theme before the week is out."

"Not if I can help it. Let's dress up and do something fun tonight." I bent forward to fluff up my hair. "Is there some party we can go to?"

He leaned over the stack of invitations on the coffee table and picked an engraved one off the top.

"We're invited to a nice dinner for France-Louisiane, if you're willing to speak French all evening."

"No, that would limit me to *oui, oui, Monsieur.*"

"So what? You used to make your living with that phrase."

Suddenly there was a *beep-beep* sound coming from the TV, then Maureen O'Boyle's picture shrank, and a bulletin came rolling across the bottom of the screen.

FRIEDA HARRIS, BETTER KNOWN AS THE PSYCHIC "MYSTIC DELPHINE," WAS JUST FOUND DEAD OF A SWORD WOUND IN HER LAKEVIEW HOME. THE POLICE SAY MURDER IS INDICATED. FURTHER NEWS AT TEN.

The message rolled across a second time. I read it again, then hoisted my big can off the couch.

"Her own home? Holy Christmas! That's my dear friend Frieda Harris from astrology class! We were very close!" I hustled out to the hallway coatrack and grabbed my mink. "Maybe I can make it over there before they cart her away."

"I appreciate your sense of loss," Julian called after me, "but why are you hurrying up to the lake to get in on a violent tragedy?"

"I'm a newspaperwoman, remember?"

"A newspaperwoman," he returned. "Only in the sense that your little gossip column, 'Uptown Tidbits,' *is* published in a newspaper. That hardly makes you a journalist within the meaning of the act."

"Not yet." I halted at the mirror to apply some Max Factor Fantasy Rose lipstick, one smear of which turns me from a drab postmenopausal matron into a raving beauty. "But wait till my byline appears on *this* little item. I'll be the local Adela Rogers St. Johns."

"At this point, you ought to settle for Lois Lane."

Frieda had lived and died in the exclusive Lakeview section of the city, up past Gentilly. I had to park two tree-lined blocks away from the fun, as there were five blue-and-white units hogging all the good spaces. I locked my car and hiked over to the scene of the crime, where yellow police ribbons barricaded the area against the buzzing, pressing throng.

Fortunately, my good friend Lt. Frank Washington was in command, standing on the front porch looking grim and official.

I jumped up and down, flailing my arms, to subtly catch his eye, and in a moment, he frowned my way and waved me through. I daintily lifted the hem of my full-cut Blackglama mink and stepped over the ribbon.

"Hey there, Frank!"

"Good evening, Margo. What is our favorite society columnist doing at a crime scene?"

"I told my editor that I knew the victim."

"And did you?"

"Well enough so it wasn't a lie. She used to sit next to me in astrology class." I climbed up on the porch to stand beside him. "Who do you think did her?"

He was jotting on his yellow pad. "At this point, my chief suspect would be Zorro."

"How's that?" I looked over his shoulder; he had drawn a diagram of a room, with distances noted in feet and inches.

"It had to be an expert swordsman." He turned a page and kept writing. "You try running a human being through with a saber. Just slicing neatly between the ribs like that, straight on through to the heart."

"It was her own sword? The one in the commercials?"

"Exactly. So it must have been unfamiliar to the killer. All the more reason to believe he knew exactly what he was doing. Did you know any of Miss Harris's friends?"

"We had a few acquaintances in common."

"Maybe you can be of some use then." He bent over and lowered his voice to the barely audible. "There's an indication that the murderer's name started with a *P*. The scene inside is pretty gory. Can you take it?"

I gave a toss of the head and smiled pertly. "What the heck."

"Come with me, then."

I didn't look around at the mob straining at the police lines (so as not to seem superior) as I followed Frank's broad back into the house. The front door opened right into the living room, with no foyer or vestibule in which to kick one's shoes off and decompress. It was a home designed to sell, not to live in. I took quick note of the monochrome wall-to-wall carpeting and hotel suite–type furniture. There wasn't a real antique or piece of art to be seen. Here was a house that new money built.

The focal point of the room was over the fireplace, a five-foot gilt-framed poster of the Mystic Delphine herself, looking beautiful and un-wrinkled. (Thanks to the taughtening of her skin through some unnat-ural means.) She held her prop sword straight out in both hands.

"We think Miss Harris was killed last night," Frank allowed. "Since today is Sunday, the office was closed and empty till the cleaning woman dropped by to pick up her rug shampooer and got a nasty surprise."

He led me all the way through to the master bedroom and stopped us at the doorway. I had missed the main exhibit. The late Mystic Del-phine, sword and all, had been trundled off to the morgue and there re-mained only a taped outline to remember her by.

"See there?" The lieutenant pointed to a disgusting blotch on the baseboard. "It seems the victim had just enough time and strength to scrawl that *P*."

It was drawn in blood, now dried and clotted. A distinctive ♇ nearly six inches high. I looked just long enough to get the picture, then turned my back.

"But that's not a *P*, Frank. What looks like a *P* with a long stem point-ing to the right is actually a combined *P* and *L,* the symbol for Pluto."

"Mickey Mouse's dog?"

"Not *that* Pluto, Sherlock. The glyph stands for the god of the underworld; the planet of sex, death, and regeneration; the ruler of Scorpio."

He sighed mightily, as most men do when you allude to astrology.

"All right, then. It's a theory." He flipped to a clean sheet of lined paper. "If she believed in that stuff the way you do, it might be a clue. When is Scorpio supposed to be?"

"About October twenty-third through November twenty-first."

"You think the deceased made that letter to implicate someone born between those dates?"

"No, I don't. If she'd wanted to indicate that, she should have drawn the glyph for Scorpio, which is an *M* with a forked tail."

"I see."

Then Frank decided maybe I was an expert witness and worth inviting for coffee. So he ushered me back outside through the murmuring, shuffling crowd, all the way to the front seat of his unit, where he uncapped a thermos bottle. "Tell me how you knew the victim."

"I met Frieda at a class in fundamental astrology." I shook my head at the proffered coffee cup but graciously accepted a jelly doughnut. "She figured she could master the subject in a few weeks, like typing. When she found out the study takes closer to a lifetime, she hung in just long enough to pick up some jargon, then dropped out."

I leaned forward to take a bite so the sugar would get on Frank's upholstery rather than my mink. "Next I heard, she was calling herself 'the Mystic Delphine' and claiming to be psychic."

He nodded. "The woman had been working the area for ten years. Bunco was watching her, but we've never been able to get her for fraud, so long as she didn't try any Gypsy 'vanishing money' tricks . . . "

At that point, a red news van hove into view, and a tall young man leaped out in full makeup, with a telegenic trench coat flapping around what looked like an Armani suit and tie.

"Must be from a local station." Frank watched the rearview mirror. "Is that Dennis? No, I've never seen him before."

"It's none other than David Ariane. You're due for the honor of meeting WLOC's new 'Generation X' reporter. Handsome as a Greek god." I ducked down and peered over the seat back. "The station has been giving him a blanket promo campaign."

Ariane began sprinting along the yellow ribbon, holding up a microphone and shouting over his shoulder to the denim-clad, gum-chewing tech who followed him with a video camera.

"I'll bet he's trying to find me." Frank brushed the sugar off his seat. "It'll be interesting to see how long it takes him."

"He's sure to locate you within hours. Ariane was known for his crack crime reporting in his last town."

"What town was that?"

"Muncie."

"Hoo!" Frank whistled. "He must have had a whole slew of scary crimes to report up there. Open containers . . . uncurbed dogs . . . "

"Evidently he lucked into enough misbehavior to get some dramatic footage of himself. WLOC offered the kid a hundred thousand a year, and they've spent a fortune touting him as 'the city's most exciting new reporting sensation.' "

"Whoop-de-do. He leaves me cold."

"You won't have time to warm up to him, either. Ariane's only dropped into New Orleans long enough to fill out his résumé on his way through to the big time."

"Dubuque? . . . Sheboygan?"

"Bangor . . . Saskatoon . . . "

Officer Duffy tapped on the window. "Frank? About Mrs. Ruiz, the cleaning woman? . . . We took her statement and sent her home."

"Good," Frank said.

"She's not a suspect," I said as a fact.

"Not unless you suspect that a ninety-pound grandmother of six rammed a sword through a woman she barely knew, then sat and watched TV for eighteen hours before calling nine-one-one."

"The blood was dry when your men got here?"

"Completely. Now, with Mrs. Ruiz out of the equation . . . " He turned in his seat. "Did Frieda Harris have any enemies or rivals that you know about?"

"Enemies? But this couldn't have been premeditated, right? I mean, nobody would walk into the house intending to kill someone with a *sword*."

Frank shrugged one shoulder. "Actually, a sword is pretty efficient. You can't get hold of a gun without the risk of its being traced. Poison may require access to the target's kitchen and is unreliable as to delivery of dosage." He took a sip of his coffee. "Try to strangle someone without her leaving any marks on you. And how do you use a knife without getting blood all over your clothes?" He recapped his empty thermos. "Yes, I approve of the sword. Neat. No forensic evidence."

I made it back home to Piety Street before ten, pulled up against the curb, guided by the helpful scraping sound, and honked. When Julian is home, he walks out to see me up to the house. But his BMW was gone, so he must have been out at the France-Louisiane thing, prattling in French with a bunch of stuck-up frogs, telling jokes about oafish Corsicans.

I had to call on my number two escort.

"Catherine! Yoo hoo! Wah wah wah!"

It took maybe thirty seconds for my four-footed bodyguard to hear my call, squeeze out of her dog door, and come galloping down the front walk, where she leapt over the four-foot iron gate in a single bound and stood on the sidewalk, wagging furiously.

Catherine is a catahoula, that blue-eyed, gray-spotted hound descended from Spanish war dogs and red wolves. They were bred here in Louisiana for herding stock and chasing rabbits through swamps.

She was the ugliest, scroungiest of street dogs when she walked me home one night nearly three years ago. I didn't mean to, but in the course of events, I ended up inviting her to move in. I was tempted to make a rhyme and call her Beulah or Tula but then, since the poor bitch wasn't exactly endowed with the gift of beauty in the first place, I decided at least to give her a beautiful name, which she has since worn proudly along with her splendid rhinestone collar.

Now after years of a generous diet of meat and fat and weekly baths with Show Dog Shampoo, the hound has actually lived up to her gracious name and become beautiful. For a catahoula, anyway.

First, I looked around to make sure there was no one on the street, then I opened the car door and, in Catherine's good company, dashed around to the trunk to retrieve my purse. I hustled to unlock the front gate, and she and I scrambled through it together. I slammed it shut, locked it behind us, and we ran up the walk and slipped into the house without incident.

"Good girl!" I patted her head. Once again, I had stretched the odds and made it home without being mugged. I feel lucky every time it happens.

2

*G*ood morning, Margo."

"Ugh. Mmf."

"My, you're bright and perky today."

"If you wanted bright and perky at this ungodly hour, you should have married Regis or Kathie Lee."

I stumbled into my chair and hunched over my empty place mat, blearing across the table at Julian's eggs and wondering how anyone's stomach could be awake at eight A.M.

"You've always resented mornings, dear. But I can lighten your mood. I heard a great joke at the France-Louisiane dinner last night."

"I'll bet it's about—"

"These two Corsicans—"

"I knew it."

"They're at the opera, see?" Julian tore his toast. "And when the soprano starts to sing, one Corsican leans over and asks the other, 'Coloratura?' So the other Corsican looks at his watch and says, 'Huit heures et demi.' Isn't that funny?"

He laughed himself to demonstrate that it was.

"Mmmpf . . . A riot. Don't you wonder what I'm doing up so early?"

"This *is* awfully unusual for you." He broke the egg yolk. "Is the house on fire? Are you in labor?"

"Much more exciting than that Neg; I've got the assignment." Catherine appeared from beneath the table and pushed her nose under my hand to make me pet her, so I talked while petting. "Felix is letting me write some background on the Frieda Harris story."

"He's favoring you over his real news reporters?"

"So far, he's only promised me a sidebar: 'An Old Friend Remembers . . .'"

" 'An old friend'? Hah!"

"Well, we might have been friends if she hadn't been such a crud."

"You have to be a bigger phony than she was."

"I will if I have to. Her office was in her house, so I'm going to tool on up to Lakeview and interview her staff."

"You think they can give you information about the murder?"

"Probably not, but I'll have a chance to get the dope on her operation." I scratched behind a furry ear. "Between you and me and Catherine, I don't care if the murderer is caught or not. I have a personal hatred for phony psychics."

"That sounds silly coming from an astrologer."

"Which is exactly our problem, Julian." I shook my unoccupied fist heavenward. "The general public puts us in the same category with those spaced-out ouija watchers and pendulum swingers. We're scientists. We don't claim any paranormal powers."

"Science is tiresome." He buttered a bite-size fragment of toast. "People would rather believe in magic. Angels and elves and novenas at the foot of Saint Jude's shrine."

"Why not? Calling on divine intervention sure beats working for a living."

"Even diabolic intervention, it seems." He poured himself another cup of Community Dark Roast. "I heard that thousands of poor suckers were putting their lives in the hands of the Mystic Delphine."

"That's because she cooked up a very elaborate stage act to convince the public that she had special powers. She talked in a funny voice and pretended to be channeling an Egyptian priestess."

"It must have been effective. Some people swore she read their minds."

14

"She read cue cards is what she read. Every trick those so-called psychics perform can be duplicated by conjurers." I picked up a teaspoon. "From bending spoons to 'thought projection.' I can do most of them myself."

"Where did you learn so much about it?"

"I used to work with Leonard the Magician at the Follies Club; that is, on the same bill. He followed me onstage."

"With a shovel?"

"With mirror boxes, Chinese rings, and collapsible bouquets." I made a bouquet of my table napkin and waved it dramatically. "I used to sneak behind the curtain and watch his act. From the rear, where I could see what he was actually doing."

"I'm sure he enjoyed your spying out all his tricks."

"I tried my best to get into the field legitimately. I even auditioned to be his assistant."

"What happened?"

"Couldn't make the weight."

Julian nodded over his cup. "He favored thin stooges?"

"Thin, petite, and limber. A magician's assistant has to fold herself up into some claustrophobically tight places." I patted my ample hips. "So I never had a chance of getting a job with Leonard."

"Don't give up yet. If David Copperfield can make the Statue of Liberty disappear, maybe he can find a spot big enough for your derriere."

"The immediate problem is getting that self-same derriere up to Lakeview to interview Delphine's employees." I slumped forward till my nose hit the place mat. "And my blood pressure's about as dynamic as deep sludge this time of the morning."

"No problem. The office doesn't need me today." Julian drained his cup. "I'm available to drive you."

" 'Yore gooder 'n' ary angel, paw.' " I covered a yawn. "Now, how do I crank up the machinery?"

"You need some chemical enhancement— Catherine! Go get Mommy a Coke."

The canine member of the family came to attention, wagged her tail at the commission, and trotted off to the kitchen. I heard her pull on the towel Julian had tied to the refrigerator door to open it, put her head in-

15

side, and take a Coke in her mouth. Then, with professional pride, she carried it back to my chair.

"Thank you, Catherine." I tilted the can away from me in case she had shaken it up, but thankfully, it didn't squirt. "Some day her big teeth are going to puncture this aluminum."

I sucked in some revitalizing sugar and caffeine and arose to meet the day.

Delphine's secretaries, Nona and Didi, were young, blond, and interchangeable. I thought they should be required to wear name tags.

I introduced Julian first and then myself with a cute embossed card featuring the paper's logo, my name, and "Uptown Tidbits" in quotes. They seemed suitably impressed.

"Gossip column." One nudged the other, and they giggled.

I told them I had a few questions and prefaced with, "I'm very sorry about your loss."

They both regarded me blankly, then glanced down at their persons, as though looking for what accessory they could possibly have lost.

"The murder must have been hard on you," I prompted.

The two shrugged in unison.

"Did you consider Miss Harris a good boss?"

They looked at each other and silently agreed upon a spokesperson. The blond on the right.

"Delphine didn't talk to us much."

"She thought she was too good for us, ya know?" added the blond on the left. "Like Leona Helmsley or a queen or something. Andrew Berry was our real boss, and he was OK."

"Yeah, it was him who ran the office. Except for the P.R.P."

The left blond nudged her. "We're not supposed to talk about that."

I was most interested in anything they weren't supposed to talk about but discreetly changed the subject. "Can you think of anyone who had a grievance against Delphine?"

The blonds looked at each other.

"How about Dr. Ingram?" asked Nona or Didi.

"That's what I was thinkin'," replied Didi or Nona. "He was pretty mad when we saw him."

I almost dropped my pad.

Julian stayed cool. "You don't mean Dr. *Harold* Ingram? The celebrated uptown surgeon?"

"I dunno about 'celebrated.' Black hair, mustache . . . "

"That's him." I didn't have to write down the name. "He did my father-in-law's prostate operation."

"Thank you for bringing that up," Julian murmured.

"Dr. Ingram consulted a telephone psychic?!"

"Nah," said the left blond. "He wasn't a client. But he came around asking to see her. He was freaked out about something."

"Crying," the other agreed. "Face all red. He didn't look so 'celebrated' in this office last week." She shifted her gum. "But that was just the latest one. There were a lot of crazy people who didn't like Delphine. Somebody was always accusing her of fraud or something. Just look in her letter file."

"We hope to," Julian said, "but I'd be more curious about the people who *did* like Delphine. With whom did she spend most of her time?"

The blonds conferred telepathically for a moment before the left one said, "That would be Sidney."

"A boyfriend?"

They giggled together. "Someone's boyfriend, maybe. Not hers."

"We'd like to talk to him."

"Someone's boyfriend" had no office of his own, but temporarily, we were told, disposed of Delphine's.

Sidney Bowers was seated at a reproduction of a French provincial desk, blocking the view of the window behind him. Bowers was bodaciously obese.

(But I wasn't supposed to think of him in that way. According to Miss Georgia's guide, he was to be described as "portly" or "of stocky build.")

He had unrolled a full-color poster of his late employer and seemed completely absorbed in keeping the edges from curling. But at the sight of us, he lumbered to his feet.

"Aren't you Margo from 'Uptown Tidbits'?!" He extended a chubby hand. "I just *love* your column!"

"Thank you." I took his hand and passed it on. "And this is my husband, Julian Fortier."

"My goodness, I've heard about you. But I never thought I'd have the pleasure."

"Don't feel left out." Julian sighed. "No one's had the pleasure in years."

"Ooh! Well, please sit down."

I looked around the office, which was decorated in ultrafemme, with little bud vases, pink rugs, and draperies offsetting furniture so scaled down as to make any male visitor feel like a hulking gorilla.

But Sidney, settling in again, looked perfectly comfortable. "Are you here about what happened to poor Frieda?"

Julian and I balanced on the edge of a spindly love seat, somewhat apprehensively testing it under our combined weight.

"I'm afraid so."

"The police have been all over this house. They've sealed off her bedroom, where it happened." He shuddered. "Not that I'd ever want to go back in there."

"It must have been a shock."

"I didn't even know if I should come in today."

"Sidney?" One of the front desk blonds stuck head and hand inside with a letter. "This is addressed to you."

She tossed it over, and Sidney tried to catch it, fumbled, then picked it off the desk and ripped open the envelope without looking. "Yes, Frieda was a real camp. I'm having a terrible problem coping with this. But I'm strong. I'll get through it all right."

"Good for you," Julian said solemnly.

I had just spied, peeking out from under the poster, a red, leather-bound address book. It had to be Delphine's personal directory. I wondered if there were some risk-free way to make it my own. I pulled my eyes back into my head and took up the conversation.

"Nona and Didi told us you were Miss Harris's closest confidant."

"That's true— Damn, this is an ad for a dating service! Where did they get my name?" Sidney put the paper back in the envelope and shoved it into the wastebasket. "She had me on the payroll as her administrative aide, but actually I was her beautician. I did it *all,* hair, face, nails."

My ears pricked up. "Then it was you who glued her lifts on?"

"Absolutely." He smoothed his pompadour. "She insisted on wearing them for every commercial and public appearance."

"Excuse my flagrant ignorance," Julian interposed, "but what kind of lifts does one glue on?"

"The kind that make a temporary face-lift," I said.

"Wait." Sidney stood up. "I'll show you on Margo." He scrambled behind me and put a set of pudgy fingers to each of my temples. "See, if I pull back here, I can tighten up a woman's whole face. Your wife would look ten years younger."

"Splendid." Julian leaned back for perspective. "Would you be willing to keep that up, day after day?"

I felt Sidney's giggle through to my cheekbones.

"That's not necessary. I can achieve the same effect by gluing a little pad behind each eye with surgical adhesive and connecting them with a tight elastic band that stretches behind her head. Then I cover the whole contraption with a wig. Voila! Instant youth."

As he made his way back to the desk, I smiled brightly to pretend I wasn't insulted.

Julian nodded. "How long had you been performing this priceless service for Delphine?"

Sidney wiggled his fingers. "As long as she'd been aging. You know, most women just can't be photographed after forty."

Julian grinned, and I shot him a look that could freeze Lake Pontchartrain (which is salt water).

Sidney babbled on. "But I'd been friends with Frieda since she first moved to New Orleans, twelve years ago. She lived in the double next to mine on Royal Street. Back then, whenever she was having man trouble, or *I* was," he simpered, "we would share a bottle of wine out on her balcony and cheer each other up."

"You probably knew her better than anyone."

"I would guess so."

"What does this mean to you?" I showed him Frank's crime scene photo of Frieda and her dying message.

"It's a *P*. No . . . " Sidney frowned. "It looks more like the symbol for Pluto." He sat stock-still for nearly a minute before reanimating. "Pluto. Of course, it's the planet of death. Funny, I never thought Frieda was that philosophical. I mean, taking all that trouble to make one final statement. Embracing the inevitable . . . "

It was time to catch him off guard. "Tell me about the P.R.P."

"The Psychic Research Project," he was distracted enough to answer. "That's a nonprofit department entirely financed by donations."

"Were there many of those? Donations?"

"Sure. Some months the P.R.P. brought in more than the phone lines."

"Some 'nonprofit,' " Julian muttered.

Sidney nodded. "They started it to study people's psychic abilities. Nona was supposed to conduct tests of the Mystic Delphine's powers and then type up the results."

"Who was supervising the tests?"

"Why, Nona."

"Just Nona?"

"And the Mystic Delphine, herself, of course."

"How was the nonprofit money distributed?"

"Most of it went into buying and keeping up the facility itself, which just happens to be this house." He waved around his head. "Then there are the four psychic subjects she keeps on the payroll."

"Four psychic subjects? What do they do, run telepathy tests all day?"

"Not exactly." He tittered. "One subject runs the lawn mower. Another runs a vacuum cleaner and the dishwasher. The third, Nona, runs the nine hundred lines. And of course the fourth, Didi, is the most psychic of all." He winked. "She runs the computer and answers the phone in the office."

"So most of Delphine's employees were being paid with project funds."

"Why not? It was her money."

"Technically, it was not."

We heard steps in the hall, and Sidney looked out the doorway and cringed. "Ooh, dearie me, here comes Andy. He's insufferable. Trouble is, he's my boss now."

Andrew Berry was a small, ferretlike man in shirt sleeves, with the beaten, frazzled look of a brothel keeper whose whores have all deserted, so that he's reduced to running the place by hand until he can hire some more.

He gave us a perfunctory nod. "You must be the Fortiers."

"We absolutely must." Julian stood and stuck out his mitt, in the posture of an affable fraternity bud.

Andrew pumped it twice. "Sidney, go box Delphine's files."

Sidney gave me a secret "Get him!" look, then bustled off to do as he was told. Julian resumed his seat next to me, and Andrew perched on the edge of Delphine's desk as though he were usually too busy to settle comfortably anywhere.

I said, "Sidney was very helpful. He seems dedicated."

"That pinwheel?" Berry picked up a memo pad and slapped it down on the desk. "The only good thing about this crisis is that I don't have to watch him swishing around anymore. I'm sick of his fruity posturing."

"Fruits!" Julian snorted. "They're trying to take over the world."

I gave him a subtle elbow. "I've been noticing that too. They seem to be everywhere. But Sidney seemed to know a lot about Frieda."

Andrew nodded sullenly. "Probably more than I did. Girls tell each other things. She forced me to put that pansy on the payroll. What could I say?" He swung his foot and kicked the wastebasket. "It was all Delphine's operation. She gave the orders, and I just tried to carry them out."

"Really? Nona and Didi implied that *you* were the brains of the business."

He moved his head from side to side. "They didn't see what was going on behind the scenes. I was just paid help like them, serving at her majesty's pleasure. She hired Sidney to give her a beauty makeover, and I'll have to admit he did that well."

"But now that she's gone . . . "

"I can't wait to get rid of him."

"Would you tell me how to reach your other employees, the ones who work the phones? I'd like to get their recollections."

"No problem." Andrew looked around the room. "But they won't be employees for long. Unless I can figure out how to run a Delphine psychic line without Delphine. Her act and commercials were the only draw we had."

"But she, herself, wasn't involved in the day-to-day operation?"

"No, I managed the business office and also produced her stage show.

She was scheduled for an appearance at the Henson Auditorium next Wednesday night." He pulled an eight-by-ten flier out of the drawer and held it up: THE MYSTIC DELPHINE SHARES HER GIFT OF VISION

"But after all this . . . " He crumpled the flier and dropped it in the wastebasket. "I'll be forced to cancel the program."

I said, "The police think Delphine tried to name her murderer."

"I wish she had."

"Does the glyph for Pluto mean anything to you?"

"Pluto?" He looked at me askance, as though I were claiming that planet for my home, then shook his head. "No, I'm weak in astronomy."

"What's your zodiac sign?"

"Virgo."

"That's a good sign for an office manager."

He wrinkled his sharp little nose. "That would have been my third or fourth choice. You see, I started out to be a classical actor in New York."

"Classical? You had formal training?"

"At the American Academy of Dramatic Arts. I studied all the great playwrights." He paused and looked for their names in the ceiling tiles. "I lost myself in Shaw, Williams, Ibsen, Sh—" He coughed. "Shirley."

Julian leaned forward. "Shirley?"

"James Shirley." Andrew smirked. "He was one of the leading dramatists of the early seventeenth century. Before the plague."

"Before the plague?"

"I graduated near the top of my class." He lifted his chin. "Did a few well-received bits in Off and Off-Off. I was nominated for an Obie for my one-man show about Abe Lincoln."

"Very impressive," I pretended aloud.

He took a slight bow. "Then I saved my pennies and bused out to L.A., figuring to get some work in films, or at least in"—here a sneer—"*television*. But I wasn't pretty enough or lucky enough. Talent and training don't mean dick out in La La Land." He couldn't act well enough to keep the bitterness out of his voice. "So I ended up playing 'Outlaw Pete' at Knott's Berry Farm. Frieda was there playing a dance hall girl. That's how we met."

"She also was bound for the stage?"

"You kidding? She never could've scored so much as a walk-on in summer stock. Couldn't get into character for shit. Whatever talent she had was limited to choosing costumes and reading cue cards."

"Have you heard about anyone threatening her lately?"

"Nothing that doesn't go with the territory. There was this school-teacher who tried to sue Delphine for fraud." Andrew went to the door and called down the corridor. "Hey, Didi! What was the name of that schoolteacher who wanted to sue us? Something Spanish!"

"Mariette Nuñez!" was hollered back.

"Nuñez, yeah. I heard she went to a lawyer, but the guy told her she had no case." He returned to the desk and sat behind it this time. "So it's possible she tried for an extralegal remedy."

"What kind of fraud was she accusing you of?"

"A prediction that didn't come true. Something like that." He snickered. "Hell, you can't sue a psychic line every time they make a wrong call. You can't take Dan Milham to court if he predicts a sunny day and it rains, right?"

"Not even if you get wet."

"So check it out. When Ms. Nuñez couldn't find satisfaction through the court system, maybe she didn't leave it at that."

"Do you have other unsatisfied customers?"

"There's bound to be a few, but we're protected by our disclaimer: 'for entertainment purposes only.' Our psychics don't *say* you can rely on their advice."

"So you never thought Delphine had miraculous powers?"

Andrew made a "Ha!" sound. "Listen, the only 'miracle' involved was what my fill lights and lens filters did for her complexion. You know, she was over forty."

"The commercials were very well done," Julian said quickly, to forestall any remark I might have made.

He nodded at the compliment.

"My greatest accomplishment was making Delphine a media star. See, we couldn't and can't afford any Dionne Warwick or LaToya Jackson as an endorser, so we worked with what we had." He glanced down at Sidney's poster of Delphine and, in a sudden angry motion, rolled it up and crushed it in his hands. "Now without our figurehead, we're out of business!"

I strove to appear sympathetic.

"Maybe a local celebrity would appear in your ads."

"I've been working on it all morning." Andrew shook his head in frustration. "I called Pete Fountain, but he wasn't interested. Archie Manning wouldn't touch us with a fork. And I couldn't even get 'Morgus' on the *phone*."

As we walked down the steps, the red WLOC van pulled up and New Orleans's "new reporting sensation," David Ariane, jumped out and landed running, the picturesque trench coat flying behind him like a cape.

I took Julian's arm. "Now you know why I had to get up so early in the morning."

"To beat Ariane down here?"

"You see? I got everybody's honest opinion about Delphine, plus a list of contacts, before he even finished dabbing on his makeup."

"I'll leave you here to enjoy him while I bring the car around," he said. "I had to park over on Jay Street." With that, Julian sprinted down the steps. He's four years younger than I and annoyingly athletic.

David Ariane passed him on the way up. The "sensation" looked me over and swung the microphone around, unsure as to whether or not I was part of the story.

"Say, aren't you Mrs. Fortier? 'Uptown Tidbits'?"

I admitted it.

"I'm so happy to meet you." He grinned boyishly, showing a telegenic overbite. "May I ask what you're doing on this hard news assignment?"

I didn't waste energy acting insulted. "Just some background." I tossed my head so my hair swung. "Frieda Harris was a very dear friend."

"Is that right?" He took a step up and leaned over me, fogging the air with his potent young masculinity. "You know, I've long been an admirer of your column. I read it every day."

"Thank you," I mewed. (It only runs three times a week.)

"But the picture doesn't show that beautiful red hair or your green eyes."

"Mainly because it's in black and white."

"Yes, and that's a shame," Ariane said earnestly. "Can we get together? I'd really like to know you better."

I drew myself up and batted my lashes, flattered at such attentions from this young go-getter who could probably be my son. "Oh?"

"Absolutely." He performed that same irresistible smile that lights up my TV screen. "Why don't we meet for coffee this afternoon?"

(Tilt! Game over!) So I just smiled back at him and said, "I have other plans."

"Maybe tomorrow then?"

"Other plans."

"Later this week?" he asked my retreating back.

"O.P."

Julian had his BMW at the curb with the motor running. He reached across and opened the door for me. "That Ariane certainly is handsome."

"Do tell."

"I got the impression that he was angling for a date."

"He might have had a shot at one too, till the yutz had the nerve to ask me out for *coffee*."

"Coffee? Wow!" Julian chortled. "He must really have been smitten with your charms. Willing to invest upwards of three dollars in a courtship. Assuming pie was included."

"Exactly." I kicked my shoes off under the dashboard and wiggled my toes. "If a guy doesn't open with at least a full meal in a fine restaurant, I know I've punched a dry well."

"He's very young." Julian took a right on Paris Road. "Girls his age *do* meet for coffee."

"Right, in jeans and a T-shirt with no makeup. They're always presentable."

"Ariane isn't used to women of vintage. He doesn't appreciate all the effort you require to look your lovely best."

"That's the point. It takes me as much prep time for a coffee date as for a lobster dinner and a musical at the Saenger. After all, I have to pull myself together."

"With hooks and baling wire."

3

*T*uesday I spent getting my column out of the way. On Wednesday afternoon, Julian got home two hours before he was due and caught me slouched in front of the tube.

"Well, well. There you are watching TV in the middle of the day. How slovenly."

"This isn't entertainment, Miss Priss; it's research. Andrew Berry offered to do anything he can to help with my investigation." I pushed the play button. "For starters, I asked for a cassette of Delphine's commercials."

The setting of the first ad was a sparkling backdrop in midnight blue. Mystic Delphine posed in front of the subtly flickering cloth. Her silvery gown glimmering soft and loose, her wig black and flowing. And her face was drawn up so tightly that her eyes slanted, thanks to Sidney's work with the lifts.

"I have the power of your future," she cooed into the camera. "Take your destiny into your own hands." A huge sapphire winked on one finger as she threw out her arms to embrace the universal continuum. "Call me anytime, and let my psychic gift bring you a vision of love, riches, travel . . . everything you ever dreamed of."

"Three-ninety-five per minute," the stentorian broadcast voice advised over the one-nine hundred number. "You must be eighteen." Then flashed the disclaimer: FOR ENTERTAINMENT PURPOSES ONLY.

Julian made a face. "At four bucks a minute, that's bloody expensive entertainment if you ask me. I could see a first-run Hollywood movie for less than two minutes of that harridan's company on the phone."

I stopped the tape. "Talking about love, riches, travel, and all, she gives the impression that she's offering those things herself. Yet the most she could give is a prediction of them, which would, presumably, come true whether she predicted them or not."

Julian sat on the arm of the couch.

"Whereas, if her people were *really* psychic, ninety percent of the callers would be told, 'No, you are *not* going to be rich. You are *not* going to have a glorious relationship. You won't get to travel any farther than Biloxi, and your children will grow up, if they grow up at all, to be losers.' "

"Never happen. No one would pay money for a gloomy forecast like that."

I aimed the remote again and restarted the tape. The second commercial rolled, featuring a different dress but the same wig, lifts, promises, and disclaimers. The later commercials, filmed the following year, were more elaborately staged, showing the Mystic Delphine out on the nighttime bayou, which furnished the ambiance of a secluded witches' coven. And by then, she had taken on a bank of employees.

"My psychics have been gathered from all over the world and were tested for the strength of their powers before they came here to answer your questions," she assured the camera.

"That's a cute gimmick," Julian allowed. "To get a job as a phony psychic, are they supposed to prove they're psychic? Or prove they're phony?"

"I heard she actually did require her employees to demonstrate their cognitive powers. She had a testing board."

"Oh, I get it. If you can fool the testing board, you can fool the paying customers."

"It also provided some cover for her incorporated Psychic Research Project."

"Did you find out what the scam was there?"

"Purely a tax shelter. Delphine established the project as a nonprofit organization so she wouldn't have to declare the donations as personal income."

The last two spots on the tape had been produced only months before Delphine's death and featured the fatal saber. She held it vertically in both hands, like a scepter.

"Let the power of the Queen of Swords be yours to help you find new strength to change your life."

She would finish by pointing it down, then up again, as though dubbing somebody a knight.

When at last the tape ran out and the screen went blue, I rewound the cassette.

"She couldn't have had that saber very long," Julian noted. "She didn't know how to hold it."

"I wonder why she got the thing at all. I never did understand why Delphine styled herself after the Queen of Swords."

"It's a character in the tarot deck, right?"

"Yes, but not the Seer of the deck. That would be the High Priestess . . . And the priestess is holding a copy of the Torah, not a sword."

"It'd take a plaguey long time to beat someone to death with a Torah."

"I'd suppose the Mystic Delphine wanted a more powerful image. But there's another factor. I was comparing Frank's crime scene photos to the poster." I pushed "Eject" and slipped the tape back into Andrew's box. "Delphine wore a big sapphire ring in all her commercials. Her secretaries told me she had it on all day, but she wasn't wearing it when she was found. There was just a white indentation left on her ring finger."

"Most women wouldn't wear a big rock like that to do housework. Did the police check her wall safe?"

"Yes, and also her jewel box, according to Frank. And every drawer and shelf in the kitchen and bathroom, under the mattress, in the toilet tanks, even behind the baseboards. The ring is gone, probably with the murderer."

"Maybe she was killed for it."

"I wouldn't think so. That sapphire was a counterfeit and Delphine's jeweler said hers wasn't even particularly good yag. It was just a show-off piece."

"Since the ring had little value, why take it?"

"Why indeed? Especially considering that if it's found in the perp's possession, it could provide enough evidence to put him in the electric chair."

"What age have you been living in?" Julian scoffed. "Murderers don't go to the chair anymore. If caught and convicted, they just have to promise not to do it again."

At three-thirty that afternoon, I had an appointment with disgruntled client number one. Her place of employment was Montegut High School, where I was directed into the girls' locker room. First I poked my head in to ascertain that no one was naked, then I addressed the only adult in the group.

"Miss Nuñez?"

"Yes?" Mariette Nuñez was about twenty-five, tall, dark-eyed, and well-rounded.

"Excuse me? I'm Margo. I called you this morning."

"Oh, yes. Come in." She addressed a squarely built young blond. "Carol, please lead the girls through the stretching exercises."

The students filed out, and Mariette offered me a place beside her on the bench.

"Now, you wanted to ask me about the Delphine line?"

She wore her phys-ed teacher's working clothes, a shirt and shorts in the school colors, blue and gold, showing off her perfectly chiseled legs. For a moment, I wondered if I ever could have looked that good in shorts, even when I was young, then turned back to my agenda. "Yes. How did you get involved with her operation?"

"Pure stupidity," Mariette admitted. "I saw her television commercials and felt that I needed the guidance of someone who had her special gifts."

"Is it a secret about what?"

"Yes." She looked embarrassed, but I just sat with my hands in my lap and nodded gently until she felt constrained to say *something* and the truth was all she could come up with.

"It was a man on the faculty here at the school. The science teacher." She shook her gorgeous head. "He enjoyed having lunch with me, always waited for me at the table before starting to eat, you know? But he just never asked for a date or anything. I found myself falling in love with him and had to know how he really felt about me." She looked down at her hands. "So I paid Delphine her private consultation fee."

"Her office told me that's three hundred smackers?"

"For a half hour. Yes. I just asked her the one question, about Ralph. Then Delphine went into a trance, and the entity who appeared said Ralph really cared for me very deeply but just had difficulty expressing himself." She wrung her hands together. "So I believed her. I was so happy I just floated down the street to my car, determined to bring the man I loved out of his shell."

"I know the feeling."

"For the next three weeks, I worked very hard at it. I continued to wait for him at lunch time. Helped him whenever he had duty after school . . . I even decorated his room. I was always there for him. Then . . . " She bit her lip. "At the Halloween party last month, Ralph had a surprise for us. He introduced the faculty to a girl he'd been seeing in Jefferson Parish and announced their engagement!" Her voice broke. "You see, he was in love with her all along. It wasn't anything about trouble expressing himself. All that time, I was *nothing* to him. *Nothing*."

"I'm sorry," I said, and was.

"But why did Delphine have to lie to me and say he cared?" Mariette's eyes were brimming. "If I'd known about that other woman, I wouldn't have made such a fool of myself. Wasted so much time . . . so much *love* on him."

I leaned forward and squeezed her hand. "Because, my dear, Delphine wasn't any more psychic than you or I, and all she could give it was her best guess."

"A guess? She tore out my heart for a *guess*?"

"Because you're so beautiful, she couldn't imagine that any man *wouldn't* love you. So she assumed this one did. There was a ninety percent chance she was right."

"You think that was it?" She pulled a tissue from the pocket of her shorts and applied it to her enormous eyes. "That I'm . . . attractive?"

"You're slurpy delicious. Your only problem is, you don't know it."

"Miss Nuñez?" the chunky blond student interrupted, standing in the doorway. "Do you want us to wait?"

"No, Carol, I'll be right out." Mariette shrugged apologetically. "I have to go now. I'm teaching an extracurricular course."

She opened the locker behind her and lifted out a long, thick pole.

"What course is that?"

"Kendo."

On Thursday, it was back to the Lakeview area, to see a living person this time. Disgruntled client number two was the big-shot proctologist.

Dr. Ingram had been expecting me, so he answered the doorbell himself and whispered, "Mrs. Fortier?"

I admitted it, and he closed the door behind us, looking furtive, his eyes shifting wildly like some sixties-era impression of Richard Nixon.

"I sent my wife out to Delchamps, so we just have a few minutes." He pointed to the living room, then took my elbow and guided me past comfortable couches and love seats, all the way through to the back wall, where he offered me a hard wooden bench to sit on, as though scared to death I would leave an indentation on his upholstery.

I held my purse out for balance and settled gracefully. Ingram took the other end of the bench with a sigh.

"This thing about Delphine . . . " He shook his head. "I don't have anything to tell you."

"I understand you held some animosity toward her."

He took a deep breath as though considering a lie, before owning up. "Only because she tried to ruin my life."

"That sounds mean," I said diplomatically. "How did you get involved with her?"

"It all started with some damnable fundraising luncheon for the Arts Council. My wife, Edna, is active in charities." He nodded to himself. "Good woman."

"I'm sure."

"That Bohemian artist, Zella Funck, was running the stupid affair, and she called Mystic Delphine in to read for the women. It was supposed to be harmless entertainment."

"But it wasn't?"

"It was a disaster!" Ingram raked his hair. "Delphine went around the room telling the women things about themselves. 'You're going to have a baby,' 'Your mother is coming to visit,' stuff like that. It was just harmless woman-talk. Okay. But then, she stopped right in front of my wife and came out with, 'I see a doctor being intimate with a twenty-year-old blond. And her initials are M. G.' "

"So Edna thought the doctor in the vision was you?"

Ingram bent over and shook his head in a way that meant "Yes."

"And were you? Being intimate, I mean."

"Well . . . " He wrung his hands.

"With a blond?"

He shrugged. "Just my receptionist, Mimi Grazuli. But I swear there was nothing serious between us; it was just about sex. A man needs that, you know."

"So I've heard. Then your wife wouldn't accommodate you?"

"Well . . . " The eyes shifted downward. "I guess she *would* have. But I couldn't with her. Not anymore. She's . . . you know . . . past it. Over forty."

"That old? Eeoo." I wrinkled my nose. "I don't blame you. How disgusting."

"Yeah." The doctor's eyes shifted up again and brightened. "But Edna's a wonderful woman. She cooks every night and keeps the house clean as a pin. See?"

I watched his hand wave around the room.

"I'll say. It looks like no one ever lived here."

"Yeah. Thanks. And she's a great mother to the kids."

"So all you want out of life is some juicy young thing like Mimi just for sex while good old Edna continues to cook and clean."

Now he smiled. "Yeah."

"Yeah. But the wicked witch, Delphine, came along and threatened your sweet arrangement."

"She would have wrecked my whole life. Edna came straight home and accused me." His voice trembled with self-pity. "So I denied it, of course, but she kept saying she believed this damn bitch with the miraculous psychic powers and that she was going to file for divorce." He looked around at the house again. "I'd lose *everything*."

"Half of everything, at least."

"Yeah. So I humbled myself. The next day I walked over to Delphine's house and begged her to take back what she said at the party. I took ten thousand dollars cash from my safe deposit box and put it right on her desk. I said all she had to do for it was tell Edna she'd been mistaken."

"She refused the money?"

He covered his face with both hands. "She just laughed and said her reputation was worth more."

"So she wasn't interested in money?"

"I don't know that she wasn't. Just last week I found a cancelled check Edna had made out to that Psychic Research Project. It was f-for . . ." He had to suck in a deep breath to get the number out. "F-fifty thousand d-dollars!!"

"Fifty grand of your hard-earned money? Geez! You must have hated her for that."

"Sure. I . . . " Then the eyes started shifting again. "But, listen! I couldn't kill her! I wouldn't have *dared* to do anything to Mystic Delphine."

"Why not?"

"Well, I mean, she was psychic, right?" He spread his palms. "She would have seen it coming."

"So that was Ingram's story?" Julian grimaced. "He's nothing but a seedy little philanderer."

"And every kind of coward, I'd say. He insisted that he'd never have the nerve to kill anyone."

"So you believed him?"

"Not without verification. He reminded me of my Granny Armaugh's good advice. She once told me, 'Niver thrust a man who asks ye ta thrust him.' "

"I thought it was mainly the gent who did the thrusting."

"She meant 'trust.' That's the way she said it. 'Never trust a man.' "

"Not bad advice, I'd allow." Julian sat back in his recliner, with a volume of the encyclopedia across his lap. After all, a man wouldn't ask for your trust if he'd already earned it. What do you think of the late Delphine now, Margo? Maybe she really was psychic."

"How do you figure that?"

"How else could she know the good doctor was cheating on his wife, and even the girl's initials?"

"Let's suppose *you* wanted to know whether Dr. Ingram was cheating on his wife. How would you go about it?"

"Me?" He went "hah," then said, "Well, I'd have to go out and hire a private detective."

"And what makes you think Delphine didn't do exactly that?"

"It would be crazy. Why would she go to all that expense just to impress someone?"

"Suppose it was a someone who, suitably impressed, would make a donation to her phony Psychic Research Project?"

"It would have to be some jaw-dropping donation."

"Would fifty grand qualify?"

"It most certainly would."

"If Delphine could turn her nose up at ten thousand bucks extortion money, tax-free, then she must have been in the habit of pulling down some humongous donations. And it might help to find out where and how."

I dug into my purse and pulled out the red, leather-bound volume. "Ta dah!"

"What's that?"

"Delphine's address book."

"Did you steal it?"

"No, I rented it honestly for two hundred bucks."

"From whom?"

"Didi the office girl."

"But she had no right to . . . "

"All is fair in crack journalism. I see you've hauled out the *Britannica* again."

"Volume nine. I was just looking up James Shirley." Julian ran his finger along the entry.

"I'm doing more contemporary research. Into Frieda's circle of acquaintances."

"Whose name are you looking for?"

"Not a name. I'm looking for numbers *without* names." I sat at the coffee table, slapped down a legal pad, and began looking up numbers.

After a moment, Julian interrupted my train of thought. "Shirley's first play, *The Schoole of Complement,* was performed in 1625 at the Phoenix Drury Lane. Before the plague." He clapped the volume closed. "Andrew was right."

"Why shouldn't he be?"

"So he wasn't lying about studying drama. But why mention someone so obscure?"

"It's called showing off."

Catherine came padding in, pushed her pointed nose under my hand, and looked up at me with her soulful blue eyes.

"What do *you* want?"

Having captured my attention, she shook agitatedly.

"What do you think? I'm made of bonzies?"

She bounced up and yipped, which meant "yes."

I reached into the box and extracted two large Milk-Bones.

"All right, but this will be all for the rest of the day!" Catherine took both biscuits in her mouth and ran off to the living room to hide them. When she first came to live with us, she would eat everything she could get as soon as she got it. But by now, she is secure enough in her territory to save for the future. She knows those bonzies will still be safe under the wing chair when she returns for them later.

Julian watched her trot by with her booty. "She conned you into giving her more?"

"Well, the way she looked at me . . . "

"My dear, she's already got a pile of bonzies in her bank under the

36

chair." He sat back and crossed ankle over knee. "At this point, that dog has a greater net worth than either of us."

"Here's another unidentified number, which makes seven. Hand me the yellow pages."

My fingers walked to the *D* for *Detective* listing. It was only six columns, and I finally found a match in the fourth.

"Here we are. This is the number of 'Jake Nesbitt: Confidential Investigations. Twenty-four-Hour Surveillance, Background Checks, Divorce, Child Custody . . . ' His motto is 'We get the lowdown!' "

Jake Nesbitt was a slim, balding man with glasses whose frames must have come off the bottom shelf of an optician's bargain package. Ideally configured for surveillance, Jake was thoroughly overlookable.

"You know I can't discuss Frieda Harris. My client's confidentiality has to be respected."

"I don't think she'll make an issue of it."

"Nesbitt's confidentiality is never breached," he droned, like a record too often played. "Not even at the grave."

"Unless you have permission from the client."

"Exactly." He took off his glasses and dangled them. "And since, in this case, the client is dead, I'll never have it."

"Not so fast, Sam Spade." I opened my purse. "Upon some crack investigating, I learned that your checks were issued not by Miss Harris personally, but in the corporate name of Delphine's Psychic Research Project."

"Which doesn't mean it's any less confidential."

"But which *does* mean your client, the corporation, is still alive." I pulled out the relevant envelope and handed it over. "While Delphine's estate is being sorted out, Andrew Berry has been appointed interim director of the project, and he wrote this letter of permission for full disclosure."

Nesbitt put his glasses back on and examined the letter carefully, even running his finger over the notary's seal.

(Suspicion was his life.)

"It's in order." He folded it precisely. "What do you want to know?"

"What can you tell me about Frieda Harris?"

"Bupkis." He looked annoyed. "She didn't hire me to investigate *herself*. All I can tell you is that her checks were good."

"All right, then. Tell me what you did for the checks."

"Standard detail." He rubbed his eye to mime how boring it all was. "When Miss Harris was engaged to do her act at a party, she'd have me spend a couple of days checking out the most prominent guests. I'd pass on the details. Then, during the performance"—the detective raised his hands and wiggled his fingers in a "hocus pocus" gesture—"Delphine would stand up and pretend to be reading someone's thoughts."

"What kind of thoughts?"

"Most of it was innocuous. 'Your daughter got a new saddlebred. Your son's been accepted into Yale.' "

"What about the less welcome revelations."

"With the scandalous stuff, Delphine would get coy, see." Nesbitt tilted back in his swivel chair. "If one of the old hens was playing 'hide the salami' with her tennis pro, Delphine'd give out just enough info so that particular woman would know it was her, right? But she wouldn't spill all the particulars. So, everyone would just be mystified and entertained."

"Maybe a woman entertained to that extent would all of a sudden get very generous and pull out her checkbook."

"Maybe. I couldn't say."

"In the light of events, did you consider that someone you investigated on her behalf might have felt threatened and turned nasty?"

"Hey, she didn't send me after any dangerous characters." Nesbitt opened his bottom drawer and dropped in Andrew's notarized statement. "It was all very harmless, you know? Just part of her act."

"But you must have seen the possibilities for blackmail."

"Not my concern. Hey, I didn't do anything illegal."

"Certainly not." I picked up my purse and stood. "By the way, did you ever kill anybody?"

"Sure." He jabbed a finger at me. "*Legally*. Back in Nam."

"So you're a military man. You must have learned how to use a bayonet."

"I seem to remember a passing acquaintance with something like that back in boot camp."

"That's a good lead, Frank. Any man who has been in the service can use a bayonet."

Frank's end of the phone line was silent for a moment. Then I heard a weary sigh.

"Not applicable, Margo. A bayonet is used differently from a sword. You hold the rifle under your arm in a two-handed grip, then you ram. Get it?"

"Two-handed."

"Whereas, with a sword, one must use only one hand, aim precisely, and put the entire weight of the body behind the coup de grace. That takes both strength and skill."

"Could a woman do it?"

"Which woman? You? No. The captain of the Tulane Ladies Fencing Team? Yes."

"How about someone in between? A woman who is very athletic in some other sport."

"To be able to run a person through, precisely through the heart, she'd have to be athletic, have an expert's knowledge of anatomy, and . . . be extremely lucky."

"How about a kendo expert?"

"What? Why do you say that?"

"No reason. I . . . uh . . . just saw David Carradine do it on TV and wondered."

"And you suspect David Carradine?"

I refused to elucidate. If the luscious phys-ed teacher, Mariette Nuñez, actually did the deed, I would consider it justifiable homicide and nobody's business.

The woman who answered the door wore an old robe of indeterminate color. She squinted one eye in challenge.

"Yeah?"

"Good evening," I lilted. "My husband and I have come to see Howie Potts."

"That's my nephew." She jerked a thumb back over her fat shoulder. "Down the hall to the left."

Howie's cluttered bedroom had barely enough space for his computer, a shelf piled high with astrology magazines, and his wheelchair, run on bicep power.

"Hi. I'm Margo Fortier, and this is Julian."

"I'm so glad to meet you, Mrs. Fortier." He shook my hand firmly enough to be genuine but not hard enough to hurt. "I just love 'Uptown Tidbits.'" He looked sly. "How about putting me in your column?"

"Tell you what." I looked equally sly. "You give me your best prediction, and I'll print it over your name. If it comes true, you'll look like a prophet. But if it doesn't, you'll look like flaked-out hair brain."

"That's fair enough. I'll make it a good one."

He gestured toward the only available seating, on his unmade bed. Julian and I seated ourselves stiffly, as though in a church pew.

"Now you tell me, Howie. What's the story with the phone psychic business?"

"Not worth your column space." He twisted in his chair. "It's mostly just people who need someone to talk to. I reassure them that everything is cyclical. This too shall pass away." He waved at his computer. "I put their chart up so I can tell them *when* it will pass away. Mercury moves out of range in a few days, Mars in a few weeks. If it's a Pluto problem"— he made a face—"I tell them how to learn to live with it."

"Pluto is the slowest planet," I told Julian.

"Yes, it would be. Just what kind of person would call a stranger to ask advice of the most intimate nature?"

"Late at night, when most of the world is asleep?" Howie sighed. "Anyone."

"They must be callers with a lot of money to throw around."

"Not always." The wheelchair turned. "I get a frightful number of calls from people on *welfare*. I know they can't afford the four dollars a minute."

"So what are they looking for?"

"Magic answers, coming from outside themselves." He pointed at his computer, which was running a Star Trek screen saver. "This one woman used to call at least once a week: 'Tell me how I can get some money to pay my rent.' So, I'm staring straight at her sixth house, and I say, 'I see a lot of opportunities for employment here.' So she goes, 'No, I don't want to go out and *work;* that takes too long. Just tell me how else I can make some money.'" He shook his head. "So finally I said, 'Buy a lottery ticket, and if it doesn't win, look for a job.'"

"So most clients just want to cry on your shoulder?"

"Cry . . . Weep . . . Moan . . . Hey, no one calls an astrologer when they've just won a million dollars! When they're happy as all get out, what am I going to tell them?"

"'This too shall pass away,'" Julian offered.

"Exactly. And they sure don't want to hear that, so they generally don't pick up the phone until they're so miserable that a promise of any change has to be good news."

"You must be making a good living at three-ninety-five per minute."

41

"Me?!" he growled deeply, like a bear. "The three ninety-five goes to the service. My cut is thirty cents a minute."

"For every four dollars generated, you get only thirty cents of it?"

"And nothing extra for overtime."

"I gather that Madame Delphine wasn't the most benevolent of employers."

"She was an eighteen-karat bitch." He slapped his right wheel. "But the only bitch in town."

"Why work for any bitch at all?" Julian asked.

"Because astrology is my only marketable skill, and the Delphine line enabled me to practice it in this room." Howie sighed. "A private consulting business is impossible. My mobility is limited, as you can see. And I can't very well invite clients over to this dump."

"You must have gathered a faithful following of phone clients."

"That's true. But there is a noncompetition clause in my contract." He gritted his teeth. "I can't set up business as a phone consultant in competition with Delphine for one year after I leave her employ."

"Now that she's dead, that particular clause may be moot."

"I knew you were going to say that."

"Can you drive?"

"Yes, I have a car fitted with hand controls."

"What's your sign?"

"Scorpio."

Due to my characteristic penchant for self-preservation, I leaned back in my seat and let Julian drive.

He put on the left blinker and pulled smoothly into traffic.

"Howie Potts. Mark one for your suspect list."

"No, not him."

"You said Scorpio is the sign ruled by Pluto."

"It is."

"And anyone who uses a wheelchair is bound to have strong arms. It would have been easy for Howie to run someone through with a saber."

"But whoever killed Delphine thrust the sword horizontally. Howie would have been below her, so the path of the sword would have been upward."

42

"Not if he went overhand." Julian demonstrated, taking his pen out of his breast pocket and holding it high overhead, like a dagger, and stabbing downward. "Or suppose he tricked her into kneeling in front of his chair. 'Oops, I dropped my pencil. Would you pick it up, please?'"

6

I expected the next telephone psychic, Martin Koenig, to be living in transcendent squalor in the rear of a midcity garage or the like, and so was surprised that Friday afternoon when his street address led me to an exorbitantly expensive neighborhood up in Gentilly. The number designated an *Architectural Digest*–type edifice looming behind a tall iron gate. I pushed the round white button, then nearly jumped ten feet at the answering crackle from a hidden loudspeaker.

"Mr. Koenig? Hello?" I told the air around me. "It's Margo Fortier from the paper."

There was a second crackle in reply, and the gate buzzed open. Koenig, in person, stepped out onto his porch to greet me.

"Well, good afternoon, Mrs. Fortier. It's nice to meet the lady behind the column."

He held a long cigar with one hand and waved me up the front steps with the other.

"I'm glad you know my work, Mr. Koenig. I hope to learn something about yours."

"Certainly. Call me Martin."

"Thank you." I would be happy to get informal with this guy. He was a bald, stocky, powerful-looking type in a bush shirt and khakis. A virile boar-hog of a man.

"Martin, you don't look like my conception of a professional psychic."

"Maybe because I'm not one. Can I offer you anything?" He showed me into his living room and held out a well-padded palm to indicate the teak-and-brass wet bar in his living room.

"Soft drink, juice, or water," I said in order of preference, so as not to embarrass a prospective host. *Everyone* at least has water.

"How about a Coke Classic?"

"You read my mind."

I looked around, craning my neck to see through doorways. There was no sign of a feminine presence and no room anywhere for children. This was the home of a single man who could afford to live his sybaritic dream in the spirit of an ascetic Hugh Hefner.

He spritzed me a fountain Coke, stronger and fizzier than the bottled product. I gulped it down. It had been a couple of hours since my last meal, and my blood sugar had plunged so low that I was about to get irritable.

Martin opened a Tuborg beer for himself.

"You don't drink at all?"

"I don't care for the taste, but I enjoy a little rum sauce on my bread pudding," I assured, just so he would understand that I wasn't a dried-out drunk in thrall to some quasi-religious twelve-step program. Actually, I never did like alcohol, not even when I was supposed to be drinking for a living back in the sixties. I never wanted my consciousness altered.

"I'm a market analyst by profession." Martin poured his beer into a stein. "I trade commodities and publish a financial newsletter. You might have seen it on *Moneyline*—'The Pluto Factor'?"

"Pluto? . . . " I didn't want to delineate the significance of the word. "That's the planet of death."

"Also the planet of investment." He knitted his brow. "Are you familiar with astrology?"

"A weensy bit. I've got Jupiter trine Uranus and sextile Mercury."

He smiled. "Good. Come on, I'll show you my setup." I trooped along after him down the hallway to his computer room. He had two IBM clones, one in each corner, feeding into a single laser printer. "I've got three astrology programs installed, all customized for commodities trading."

There were graphs taped up to every available space on the north wall. He pointed to the most prominent of them and used the end of his cigar to trace its red line, which traveled upward in a jagged path. "This shows Pluto traveling toward its perihelion for the year." He cocked his head. "You know what that means?"

"Closest position to the Sun."

"Good." He tapped the graph. "Forty-five days before, I buy gold. Then ten days before it hits, I liquidate the position. When it reaches absolute perihelion, I go short. Then ten days before it hits the aphelion, I cover the position."

"After buying and selling, what's the percentage you make on your capital?"

"After a good cycle, about fourteen percent. Not much, I know. It takes a lot of trades to make a profit, but then I *do* a lot of trades."

"You seem to be doing pretty well."

He put the cigar back in his mouth and folded his arms. "I pay my bills."

"So why did you stoop to working for Madame Delphine's psychic line?"

"Research. I wanted to do a study on horary predictions. What better way than to interact with querents on a nightly basis? The feedback was immediate. When I was right (usually) they called back to say so. When I was wrong, they called back even quicker. And I learned from the mistakes, adjusted my calculations."

"Did you work from here?"

"No." He hesitated. "I chose to man the lines in the office."

"Since you're admittedly not psychic—"

"Not a bit."

"—how did you pass Delphine's famous 'psychic sensitivity' test?"

"It was a cinch." He spread his hands. "The testing board handed me their natal charts, and I told them about themselves. I guess I was accurate enough."

"How did you fit in with the actual psychics?"

"At first, I was rather patronizing," he confessed. "I figured that here I was, into a science, and they were just a bunch of delusional flakes. But in time, I realized that those people were sincere in their practice and some had real ability. I worked with a left-brained science, and they achieved the same results with their right-brained intuition." He smiled. "I had my laptop, and they had their tarot cards and amulets."

"Did you like them?"

"More than that, I found myself feeling sorry for them. You ought to meet those people. Especially Clarise. Most nights, she had to work from her home. She's so sensitive and vulnerable, it's like she's missing a layer of epidermis."

I nodded an agreement. "The gift of speech enables us to communicate only as much as we want known. Our being shielded from the true thoughts of others is a blessing."

"And essential to the science of manners."

"Which category would you put Delphine in? Left or right brained?"

"No brained," he snapped. "No science, no intuition. The woman was a complete fraud. She could never have passed her own psychic sensitivity test."

"So Delphine never answered the office phone lines?"

"She wouldn't even stay in the same room with the real psychics. She was afraid they would see through her." He tapped his brow. "They already had."

"So, the only magic she did for the operation was to make customers appear."

"That's all she *could* do. Everything Delphine did publicly to demonstrate her so-called power was a stage trick. But it was good advertising. She made those phones ring."

"Can you think of anything about her personal life that would help with my investigation?"

"I wouldn't know. She remained remote from all of us." Martin snapped his fingers. "Say, if you really want the lowdown on Delphine, why don't you look up Randall Jooby?"

"You mean the 'Baffling Jooby'? I've heard of him. Isn't he a magician?"

"He makes some kind of a living as a third-rate convention magician. But he gets more ink as a 'debunker' of claimants to the paranormal."

"How does he figure in?"

"Jooby was writing an exposé of psychic phone lines for some magazine. He sidled around the place for two weeks looking for proof that Delphine was a fraud. He attended all her performances, notebook in hand."

"You think he found the proof he wanted?"

"Why not? A reasonably intelligent high school student could have seen through her illusions. A professional magician should have doped the whole scam out after one show."

"Why did he spend two weeks then?"

"You tell me."

"Did you find Jooby threatening?"

He looked genuinely puzzled at the notion.

"How could he be?"

"He's made it his life's work to discredit your discipline."

"Hardly." Martin curled a lip. "Jooby never tried to debunk a real astrologer; he knows we're out of his league. It's the fools in the purple turbans he goes after. Or if some poor mental case goes stumbling down the street raving that he just rode a spaceship to Venus, *that's* the guy Jooby will expose as a fraud." He stopped short. "Let's change the subject. What would you say to some Viennese pastry from La Marquise?"

"I would say it makes life worth living." I followed him into the kitchen and pulled a stool up to the counter.

My host took an orgiastically large white box out of his refrigerator and cut the string with a carving knife, thank heaven. I was grateful that I didn't have to sit there faint with sugar deprivation until he managed to untie the little bow.

"Name your favorite: eclairs, cream puffs, mocha almond layer cake—"

"That one," I interrupted, bouncing on the stool.

"Mocha almond." He put it on a plate for me, served himself an eclair, issued us both forks, and joined me at the counter.

"I've been studying astrology for ten years." I used my fork to cut off a modest mouthful. "But some of my friends think it's all hogwash, and I just can't convince them it works."

"Why in hell would you want to?"

"Timing events correctly would make their lives easier."

"Sure it would." He had to use a serrated knife on his eclair. "Listen, do you know what *occult* means?"

"It means 'hidden.' "

"Exactly. And the techniques of our discipline have been hidden for a good reason. You think I'd make any dough on my trades if everyone was using astrology? Hey, *someone* has to be buying when I'm selling."

"That sounds greedy and selfish to me."

"Knowledge of this science is better than gold, Margo. You don't give away gold."

"You do if there's enough for everybody."

"Then it would be devalued." He chewed and swallowed. "In ancient times, if you wanted to learn the secrets of astrology, you had to apprentice yourself to a master, effectively become his slave for some twenty years, and just hope he would be kind enough to tell you all he knew, bit by bit, before he died."

"I know we're lucky to be living in this age," I said. "All we have to do nowadays is read some books."

"Doubly lucky to have access to the books." He smiled, and there was a dimple in his right cheek. "The high muck-a-mucks in the Vatican had the right idea. They condemned the study for the faithful, while building for themselves the most extensive astrological library in the world."

"They kept it to themselves."

"So let's keep it to *our*selves, Margo." He lifted his glass. "To ourselves."

I lifted my own glass. "Mazel tov. That means 'good planets.' "

"I know." He clinked his glass against mine. "By the way, I like redheads."

"And I like big fa . . . " In a millisecond, I flashed on Miss Georgia. " . . . uh . . . fabulous brown eyes, like yours."

He smiled again. "Good."

Frank put on his reading specs to study the list.

"This Martin Koenig worked Delphine's psychic line with a computer?"

"Right. He and Howie Potts answered the callers' questions with horary charts."

"What's that?" Frank sounded suspicious.

"Spelled with an *H* not a *W*," I hastened to assure him. "It means 'hourly.' A horary chart shows the planet positions for the time a question is asked."

"You can derive a plausible answer from that?"

"Astrologers have been deriving them for some five thousand years."

"So Koenig calls his newsletter 'The Pluto Factor'?" Frank drummed his fingers on the table. "Then Delphine was very possibly pointing us in the direction of your millionaire financial analyst."

"No, I don't think he did it."

"Yet, from the way you describe him, he certainly had the physical strength."

"Strength, yeah. Great biceps. He must work out." I thought about the biceps for a moment, till Frank's reproving look brought me up short. "But—uh—no motive."

7

*T*he semifamous magician, Randall Jooby, had conveyed that he would be pleased as punch to spend his Friday night being interviewed by the "Uptown Tidbits" columnist and invited me to meet him in his Frenchmen Street home at nine P.M. He had left the porch light on.

I paused to check my lipstick in the rearview mirror in order to make the best first impression and then, in that interest, recalled Miss Georgia's third dictum: "Pay a compliment if you can."

Okay, now I had to think of a good compliment. Jooby's most outstanding feature was his luxuriant toupee, a monochromatic brown brush as sleek as a mink pelt, which must have cost him a fortune. It was obviously his pride and joy, so I decided to compliment him on that.

Maybe I'd say, "My, that's a very handsome toupee. Where did you buy it?" Or, "Gee, your toupee looks just like real hair."

There had to be some examples of appropriate compliments in Miss Georgia's guide, so I got it out of the glove compartment, turned on the dome light, and opened the book to the glossary. *Toupees,* page 73.

I turned to page 73: "There is no such thing as a toupee," it blared in bold type. "No matter how obvious it seems, even if a gentleman's hairpiece *peels off in your mouth,* it is never to be alluded to."

Oh, nuts!

All right, then. I had to come up with something else to compliment.

He appeared as a squat shadow inside his screen door.

"Good evening, Mrs. Fortier. Welcome to my home."

"Charmed, I'm sure."

Once inside the dimly lighted foyer, I got a good look at him. My host affected a black ascot over black lounging pajamas and a flowing black silk smoking jacket. The "Baffling Jooby" managed to baffle me as to where he'd gotten his taste in clothes.

"So," I said cheerfully, "Bela Lugosi *did* leave an estate."

Jooby issued a thin smile. He had enhanced his macabre illusion by cultivating a Mephistophelian pointed goatee and waxed mustache.

"You might say I live my work. I've been preparing for a charity function at the Black Hat Club this weekend."

He showed me through the hallway, waving sleeves so wide that I feared they might have been concealing some wretched live varmint to bring forth at the drop of an abracadabra.

My host's living room was illuminated with only a single low-watt bulb and looked like a magician's warehouse, with garishly painted illusion boxes, a gimmicked guillotine, multicolored streams of silk scarves, and Chinese rings.

"It was so kind of you to see me," I gushed.

"My pleasure."

Oops! I'd almost forgotten. Now it was time for the compliment.

"My goodness, what a great nose job! Who did it for you?"

He clapped his hand over the subject, and his eyebrows moved up and down while he decided whether he could fake me out, maybe claim it was stock from the factory. No.

"Well, I . . . uh . . . broke it playing sports in college. So I had to have surgery."

"And it just naturally came out looking like Warren Beatty's. I can dig it."

No man ever had a nose job merely to look better. It was always to correct some horrendous injury sustained in some macho endeavor. But

I'd bet my new Wonder Bra he carried Beatty's picture to the hospital with him.

"This is a special privilege, Mr. Jooby. As I understand it, you are the country's most prominent 'debunker.'"

"In all modesty." He steered me to a black velveteen settee, then lowered himself into a Victorian armchair that might have been a model for a Charles Addams cartoon and launched into his usual self-promotional spiel by rote. "I make it my avocation to ferret out phony psychics who bilk the public by using standard conjurer's tricks."

"So in that spirit of an investigative reporter, you were looking into the Mystic Delphine's operation."

"'Racket,' is the word *I* use. Yes, hers along with several other of those phony psychic lines. I was commissioned to write an exposé on them for *Skeptic's Monthly.*"

"I found that issue in the library. So what did you learn about Delphine?"

"Learn?" He snorted. "What I already knew—that she was a total fraud."

"No doubt. But I read your article, 'Phone-y Psychics,' all the way through, and there wasn't a word about Mystic Delphine."

"That's because she's only local." He flicked a hand. "When I made the final edit of the piece, I decided to concentrate on the big-time national advertisers."

"That sounds perfectly reasonable. By the way, do you know how to use a sword?"

"Do I?" With that, he whirled out of his chair amid a flutter of silk, strode over to a red-lacquered box, and drew out a particularly vicious-looking scimitar. "I got these out for the charity show I'm doing at the Black Hat Club." He hefted it in his hand. "I used to stick a dozen of these into the pliant and trembling young body of my beautiful assistant, four shows a day on the Vegas strip."

I got to my feet. "They're collapsible, right? Or rubber or something."

"Ah, we have a disbeliever in the audience . . . " Jooby reversed the sword to offer the handle. "See for yourself."

I stepped over and carefully ran my fingers along the blade. "No, that's solid tempered steel, all right. And sharp enough to shave a cat."

He nodded. "The public is very sophisticated these days. They've seen every trick a dozen times on TV. You can't fool them with rubber swords."

"You know, I sensed a raging jealousy in Jooby."

Julian, being absorbed in some task involving crayons, typing paper, and scissors, answered distractedly.

"Hmm? For what?"

"How much, would you say, can an honest journeyman magician pull down these days? Assuming he doesn't have jungle animals to play with or hundred-thousand-dollar illusions?"

"I can't even guess," he mumbled, selecting a bright blue crayon.

"Could his income even compare to that generated by a phony TV psychic?" I held up my notebook. "A psychic with three hundred dollar consulting fees and a bank of sub-psychics working for her?"

"Then I guess 'No.' "

"Not even in the same stratosphere. So that was it. He was murderously jealous of Delphine."

"No sale, Margo." Julian shook his head one-two-three. "Most people make more money than I do, but I'm not petulant enough about the matter to go around killing them left and right."

"But Jooby may have had another reason to liberate Delphine from the bonds of the material world."

"What?"

"I don't know yet, but maybe for the same reason he didn't mention her in his exposé."

"He explained that." Julian picked up his scissors. "He told you it was because she's only local."

"He knew she was only local when he spent two weeks of his life auditing her shows. So why did he change his mind?" I held a finger up. "One: What if he found out Delphine wasn't really a phony?"

"We know that couldn't have been the case. If *you* saw through her tricks, a professional magician would have no problem."

"Agreed. Second possibility: Suppose Jooby fell in love with Del-

54

phine, or for some other reason didn't want to hurt her reputation?"

"I think we can rule that out." Julian began cutting out one of his colored figures in an intricate curve.

"Yes. He strikes me as the quintessential confirmed bachelor, the kind of man who never had any passion for any woman, no matter how attractive, or any thought in his life except for himself."

"He didn't come on to you, did he?"

"No. Which brings us to the third and final possible reason: Himself. It was somehow in Jooby's own best interest *not* to expose her as a fraud. And I have to find out why."

"I'm sure you'll mull that over at your leisure. But tell me how he does it."

"Does what?"

"What you described. Stick all those swords through the beautiful, pliant, young assistant without hurting her."

"They're identical twins," I suggested. "He only sticks the swords through one, then the other twin, who is still alive, comes out unhurt and takes the bows."

"He must pay his assistants very well."

"He'd have to. Tomorrow is Saturday. I have a meeting with one of Delphine's psychics, Clarise Valera. By the way, what is that you're drawing?"

"This is my new invention." He added a curlicue of azure. "You see, I cut out these lovely butterfly wings. Then we simply apply a piece of double-faced tape to the undersides"—he held out the tape—"so we can attach them to the backs of our roaches and bring the beauty of a fresh spring meadow right into our own kitchen."

"Oh, is that so? Listen, Julian. If I got hold of a roach, I'd kill it."

"Then what would be the point of the wings?"

"I can't imagine. I've got to call Frank."

I went into my office and rolled the Rolodex. The good lieutenant had given me his private number, so it rang on his desk in the Homicide Bureau. He answered on the first ring.

"Make my day."

"It's Margo. I've been cogitating on Delphine's P.R.P. You see, she collected huge tax-deductible contributions for her Psychic Research Project, which was supposed to be researching paranormal powers. But it seems the only 'power' she was researching was her own."

"Why tell me? Tax evasion is a federal matter."

"But not extortion. Maybe it gave someone a motive."

Julian poked his head in the doorway.

"How about bunny suits for the rats?"

"No!"

*M*argo, this is Clarise Valera."

Martin had his hand on her shoulder. The girl's waist-length hair was blond, and her eyes were blue and slanting, and so large that she looked like a beauty from another planet.

"How do you do?" I said.

She nodded shyly and didn't reply.

"Clarise is a triple Pisces," Martin explained. "The psychics told me she was the most gifted one on the line."

"Triple Pisces?"

Not another planet after all, but another element. She was a mermaid.

Moving smoothly as liquid, Clarise coiled into Martin's wing chair, taking the lotus position.

(Which I myself couldn't achieve without breaking at least one leg.)

"Do you mind if I . . . ?" She held up a pack of Marlboros. Martin hastened to furnish a large pewter ashtray, and she lit up a cigarette and inhaled all the way down to her long bare toes. "I'm exhausted. My son's tuition is due, and I've been working the phone lines sixty hours a week."

"You couldn't have been making too much with Madame Delphine."

The mermaid tossed her head, throwing her mane of silken hair first to one side then to the other.

57

"Three hundred in a good week."

"Considering your talent, why didn't you go into the clairvoyant business for yourself?"

"I couldn't start a phone line. It wasn't allowed."

"There was a noncompetition clause in the contracts," Martin put in.

"Yes, Howie Potts told me about that. But you could consult with people in person."

"How could I do that?" Clarise's light blue eyes were steady behind a mist of smoke. "Should I sit down in Jackson Square with an upturned milk carton and my tarot deck, behind a little sign that says 'Readings Ten Dollars.' "

"You'd make more money."

"But I would have to go out in public and deal with crowds. I'm not very good at that."

"Clarise absorbs too much psychic static from the people around her," Martin interpolated. "She's so sensitive, she can't even listen to music."

"However softly it's played, the bass line is still too loud," she murmured. "It hurts inside my brain."

She reached under her shirt and brought out a silk-wrapped parcel. "These are my cards. I always carry them with me to keep the energy pure." She untied the knot of silk, shuffled the Rider-Waite Tarot deck, then spread it out on the coffee table in an easy gliding motion. "Pick one."

I put out my left hand and tapped a card with my ring finger.

Clarise held it up. "The Magician."

"Neat. Maybe I'm going to have an affair with Siegfried or Roy."

"No, no!" She shook her waterfall of hair. "I see someone trying to manipulate you." She closed her eyes and held the card in the palms of both hands. "Someone dangerous . . . "

"Dangerous?" Martin looked alarmed.

"Well, well," I said brightly. "I'll just watch out then."

Clarise was still curled up in the chair when Martin walked me out to my car. "What do you think?"

"Is she really clairvoyant?"

"Even more than clairvoyant. She seems to be precognitive."

"What's the difference?"

"It seems there are several kinds of psychic talent," Martin said. "Clairvoyance means seeing things that are happening outside the range of a person's own natural senses. If one twin experiences something that's happening to his fellow twin across the country, that's clairvoyance."

"I've heard anecdotes about it, but no scientific documentation."

"There's also telepathy, reading minds."

"Nothing paranormal about that, Martin. When a guy says he loves me, I can tell he's lying by the unnatural strain of his voice and the way his eyes move. So he thinks I've read his mind."

He smiled. "That phenomenon is often read as 'women's intuition.' Psychokinesis is being able to move an object with the power of one's mind."

"That's purely a stage act. They use fishing line or electromagnets."

"Maybe they do. Precognition is knowing what's going to happen before it happens. That's the gift they say Clarise has."

By then, we had reached my car. I dug into my purse for the key. "If that girl is so enlightened, why does she smoke? Isn't she hip to lung cancer?"

"Her enlightenment is spiritual not physical. You would be surprised how many of these sensitives smoke to keep themselves grounded. I've been telling her to just rub a stone like the Native Americans."

"She's a great beauty."

"Ethereal."

"Are you like . . . ?" I stuttered to a halt with the key in my hand, then started up again. "Are you going with her?"

"With Clarise?" He squinted. "Are you nuts? That would be like fucking a hummingbird."

"Then she's not your type."

"I'm not a boy, and I'm not attracted to girls." I unlocked my car door, and he opened it for me. "I'll take a grown woman any time."

"Oh?" I gracefully seated myself behind the wheel. "And about how big would you like her to have grown?"

"Into an armload at least. And it might help if"—he looked me over—"she had red hair and green eyes."

"A fine color scheme."

"You're very feminine, you know? —Look it, anyway."

"Well," Julian crowed, "we've finally got a motive for Martin Koenig."

"How do you figure?"

"He seems very protective of Clarise and the other psychics on the line. He might have been angry at the way Delphine was exploiting them."

"So he'd organize a strike. That's his style. He's just too manly to kill a woman."

9

*O*n Sunday, I went to interview someone who was willing to speak ill of the dead Delphine, a conveniently disgruntled ex-employee.

Dan Aparisi let me into his house wearing jeans and a black T-shirt with the sleeves rolled up. "You're Mrs. Fortier?"

"None other."

"Umph."

He led me into his living room, and we settled on the couch.

"I work for the city of New Orleans, the Sewerage and Water Department." There was pride in the assertion. "It will be ten years in May."

"Then you didn't need a job with Delphine."

"Certainly not. I signed on with her for two months. I wanted to further my study of the *Book of Changes* and help people at the same time."

"Do you believe you have paranormal powers?"

"Not at all. I used the *I Ching* hexagrams to answer callers' questions."

He drew open a drawer in the side table, and pulled out a long hollow cylinder with wooden sticks poking out of it. "Each stick has a trigram. Two together make a hexagram, and that constitutes the means to answer any question."

"Can I ask something?"

"Very well." He shook the cylinder.

"OK, here's one. Will I find a rich, virile lover this year?" I asked, actually having a candidate in mind.

Aparisi frowned at the triviality of the matter (maybe he was expecting me to ask about peace in Bosnia or something), then bent over the table and shook out his sticks.

"At first we have *Pi,* water above earth, which means 'union.'" He looked scandalized. "Why, you already *have* a relationship!"

"Yeah, but that's just with my husband."

"He's the one you should keep. Your husband is your soul mate, your support."

"Uh-huh."

Aparisi pointed at the accusing sticks. "The second hexagram is *Kuan,* wind over earth, or 'contemplation.' You may have an affair with another man, but it would be unstable and wouldn't last."

"What news? They never do anyhow!"

Aparisi glowered at the shameless adulteress and, in a final gesture, put his precious can of sticks away in the drawer.

"Is there anything else I can do for you Mrs. Fortier?"

"Yes. Tell me why you quit Delphine."

"I didn't like the way she did business. Just watching and listening. Understand that I'm sure the psychics on the line were sincere in their beliefs. They had real compassion for the callers. But Delphine . . ." He growled. "She ran the business side like a pure hustle."

"It couldn't have taken you two months to figure that out."

"You'd think?" He sighed. "For a while, I was able to fool myself that we were doing more good than harm. I know I brought solace to *my* callers."

"When did you learn otherwise?"

"The last straw was what they did to Harriet Rosen."

"I don't know the name."

"Harriet Rosen was a seventy-nine-year-old maiden lady, very rich from West Bank real estate. Delphine ran across her at an uptown society thing and saw a natural mark. I learned all this after the fact, you understand."

"Of course."

"First she set Jake Nesbitt to find out some weakness Miss Rosen might have had. Some area of vulnerability."

"I've met Jake. I'll just bet he came up with something."

"Yes, he did. The lady's mother, Patience, had died of fever in the Influenza Epidemic of 1916, when Harriet was just a little girl. So she was always trying to contact her. She would pay anything, right?"

"I guess," I said into my notebook.

"Delphine decided she could get the most money out of the poor woman by staging a phony séance. So she found a photograph of Harriet's mother in the newspaper's morgue, and then she flew in this actress she knew from New York."

"What actress?"

He waved the question aside. "I didn't catch the name, just a bit player. I only saw her once, when they were sneaking her through the kitchen."

"OK."

"Then she must have had a wig and costume made. And I guess Delphine was an expert with makeup too, because somehow she fixed the actress up to look exactly like poor Harriet's mother!"

"How did you know all this?"

"I used to stretch my legs between calls, walk around. We weren't supposed to go into the residential wing of the house, but I was curious. I heard her setting the stage. You know what a mirror box is?"

"Yeah."

"That's how she introduced the actress. There was a vase of white roses on a pedestal, and it seemed to turn into Patience Rosen, still young and beautiful."

"Nice effect."

"The stunt worked. Poor Harriet believed she was looking right at her dead mother. The next evening, she donated a hundred thousand to the Psychic Research Center. That was tax-free to Delphine."

"That was some expensive private show."

"What's more, she made it a long-running series. Whenever the old lady got lonely, Delphine would set up the charade again, fly the actress in, and let Miss Rosen visit with her 'mother.' I didn't find out till she'd been at it for six months."

"Why didn't you go to the bunco squad?"

"With what?" Aparisi threw his arms out. "I had no video tapes of the performance. I figured the old woman was too senile to know what was going on, and she had no relatives to approach about it. If there had been an investigation of Delphine's racket, I would have stepped forward to tell what I knew, but no one at all was looking into her activities. So all I could do was get the hell out of the business."

"I understand that you were the only employee who quit because of the swindle."

"Most psychics are so spacey . . . " He swatted at an imaginary moth. "They want to believe everybody's a pure soul. They didn't focus on what was really happening. But I did." He shuddered in disgust. "It made me want to get back to my nice clean sewers."

10

"Hey, Julian? Dan Aparisi gave me a scrumptious new angle on the case. Delphine used conjurer's tricks to cheat an old spinster out of her fortune. They made a vase of roses seem to turn into the old woman's mother."

"How on Earth could they do that?"

"They'd gotten hold of an old light-and-mirror box."

Julian looked vague. "A what?"

"It's just a booth with two compartments right and left. When you open the curtain, the light is on the pedestal with the roses behind a sheet of glass in the right compartment. So that's all the audience sees. Then you gradually dim the light on the roses and bring up the light on the actress in the facing left compartment. With the light behind it dimmed, the glass in front of the roses will no longer be transparent, but will become a mirror reflecting the actress. It looks like a gradual transformation."

"Spooky."

"All it cost Delphine was the five thou she shelled out to the actress. Mainly for keeping her mouth shut. The rest was gravy."

"That sounds very actionable."

"But who was going to make the complaint? The old woman, Harriet Rosen, was a spinster and didn't have any descendants. And thinking she was visiting her mother made her happy."

"So the scam artist might rationalize."

"Delphine would claim they did her a favor. Anyway, Miss Rosen was lucky enough to die of old age around the same time she ran out of money. So she never felt the pinch of poverty."

"The phone is ringing."

"So it is." I squinted at the caller ID box and didn't recognize the number, but the voice on the answering machine was David Ariane's. I picked up.

"Are you doing anything?"

"Always."

"If you can tear yourself away, I'll show you some basic differences between the hard news beat and . . . " He paused. " . . . what *you* do."

"I can't wait."

"Meet me at the Attila Club in the Irish Channel in two hours."

The Irish Channel is an old, blue-collar neighborhood uptown between Magazine Street and the river.

Julian gallantly offered to drive me, which meant I didn't have to wear shoes in the car.

We passed a purposely quaint little strip mall, then the scenery took a turn for the very worse. I jumped out of the car before it was fairly parked, beat Julian up to the Attila Club, and pushed open the sticky door. It was a dingy local bar that looked as though no woman had ever been inside the place. Certainly not to clean up.

David was on the first stool, looking about as out of place as I felt.

"Mrs. Fortier?" He smiled over his draft beer.

"Good afternoon. I'd like you to meet my husband, Julian."

"Hello! And *I'd* like *you* to meet Butchie Muldoon." He waved across the bar. "He has been manning the taps here for twenty-eight years."

Butchie nodded modestly at the distinction, as though it were nothing at all.

Ariane reached across a row of glasses and punched his arm.

"Now, Butchie, tell the Fortiers the story you told me."

"Okay." The bartender took a big gulp of air and began. "It was like three o'clock inna afternoon. There was this raggedy punk came in, not a regular; fact, I never seen him before. But he didn't smell bad, so I served him what he wanted. A Miller Lite and a glass of ice."

Julian cocked his head at that. "A glass of ice?"

"Like the beer wasn't plenty cold enough, see? So then he went and sat on that stool over by the winda, and I forgot about him. After a while he started actin' strange. There was some flies buzzin' around on the winda, right?"

"Right," I agreed. "I'm certain there were."

"Yeah, just like now. Different flies a course. They don't live too long. So after a while I see the punk, he just grabs one a' the flies offa the winda and pokes it in his beer. The punk musta been a mental case, right? I mean, I seen a lotta guys sit here and take flies *outta* their beer, but who the hell would put one *in*?"

"I'm sure he had his reasons," I said.

"So he just keeps pokin' the fly down there till the thing drownds, then he picks it out real careful and lays it on the bar. Well, I was mad 'cause I'd have to wipe it up with this bar rag here." He flapped the very bar rag he would have employed.

"But at the same time, this woman happens to run in to use the phone, and I recognize her right off. It's that Delphine the psychic from the late-night TV commercials."

Ariane was nodding eagerly. "Delphine, yes. See?"

"Yeah," Butchie continued. "Then she goes right up to the punk and says, 'Shame on you! You shouldn't kill poor helpless creatures.' So the punk says, 'Hey, you're the Mystic Delphine,' all sneerin', right? 'Why don't you bring it back to life, then?' So she says, 'Okay, I will.' Then she pulls a little pack of sugar outta this bowl here and walks over to the guy. He's just like laughin' like she can't do it. But then, she just opens this packa sugar and dumps it on the dead fly, completely buryin' it." Butchie leaned over the bar for the punch line. "And you know what?"

I nodded. "The dead fly got up, flapped its little wings, and flew away."

"Hey! You heard the story, huh? Yeah, it happened right here." He pointed to a framed color photo behind him. "Next day, she sent me that picture, autographed with love to Butchie."

Thus insuring that the tale would be told nightly in that bar forever more.

Ariane gave me his anchorman smile.

"So what do you say to all that?"

"Heavens."

He almost fell off the bar stool. "That's it? Just 'Heavens'?"

"To Betsy. Heavens to Betsy."

David laughed, wagging his impeccably groomed head.

"Now, Margo, don't go thinking you can scoop me on this story. My interview with Butchie has already been taped and edited. See you on the Six."

"Yeah, the Six."

We exchanged waves, and the city's most exciting new reporter strode manfully out the door to the WLOC van.

Julian preceded me outside to the BMW and unlocked my car door. I slipped in daintily, according to Miss Georgia's dictum number thirty-five: "When entering a car, sit down facing outward, then turn gracefully in your seat to face the windshield. Knees always together, ladies, *please*."

I leaned over to unlock Julian's door. "Well?" he said, settling behind the wheel. "What do you say to Ariane's story?"

I cackled happily. "He can have it all to himself."

He shifted into gear and pulled away from the curb. "You think the bartender made the whole thing up?"

"No, he hasn't the imagination. He saw exactly what he said he saw."

"Then how do you explain what happened?"

"Let me answer that question with another. What was Delphine doing in Butchie's bar?"

"As he said, she just stepped in to use the phone."

"All of a sudden, she was so desperate for a phone that she stopped at *that* crummy dive? We saw a yuppie strip mall only two blocks away. No, Julian, it had to be that particular bar because it was the only one around that had what she needed."

"What was that?"

"Flies on the window."

"Huh? Oh, that's crazy."

"Who do you think was that convenient derelict Butchie had never seen before or since?"

"Just your generic derelict."

"More like a stock company derelict. Or how about our friend Andrew Berry dressed *up* as a derelict." I pulled off my shoes. "The whole event had to be staged. Remember, Butchie said he recognized Delphine right away."

"Why shouldn't he? She was on TV almost every night."

"On TV fixed up for TV, with a professional makeup job, lifts, and all. You think she usually got stretched and painted like that to go grocery shopping at three o'clock in the afternoon?"

"Some women do. But I'll concede that most don't."

"This one did this time because she had to be recognized. She was staging a performance."

"That's possible, but what about the resurrected insect? You think they got some kind of mechanical fly?"

"No, the fly was real. Why do you think the 'derelict' ordered a light beer, which is mostly water anyway, and then loaded it with ice?"

"That does seem uncharacteristic."

"He was diluting the alcohol so it wouldn't poison the fly."

"But the fly was dead."

"No, it wasn't, Neg. That's my point. The fly was just waterlogged. So Delphine sprinkled sugar on it, which is about the driest substance you could put your hands on. It soaked up all the beer, and the little bastard simply dried out, spread his dirty little wings, and went on about his business."

"How did you learn all that? Another trick from Leonard the Magician?"

"No, it's just an old bar hustle. Usually involves a bet. 'I bet I can bring it back to life . . . No, you can't, either. Where's your money?' I can't imagine how Butchie could have been in the bar business all those years and never seen it. Maybe it's a northeast thing."

"So as soon as Butchie mentioned the fly, you knew the whole setup."

"Yep."

"But you didn't tell David Ariane."

"Nope."

Then Julian cackled.

Once inside the house, I headed straight for the answering machine as usual. There was only one message, from my contact in the late Delphine's operation, Andrew Berry. I dialed right back.

"Oh, Margo? Guess what? I didn't have to cancel the show at the Henson Auditorium after all!"

"You're going to have a Delphine one-woman show without Delphine?"

"Not exactly," Andrew crowed. "There will be a slight change of cast. Sidney Bowers is going on for Delphine."

"Sidney? But I thought you were raring to get the guy out of your life. What made you change your mind?"

"He's great! You'll see for yourself at the show. I'm leaving two tickets in your name at the box office."

"Thank you. We'll certainly be there."

"Better pick them up early. I expect to be S.R.O. by curtain time."

*A*s the curtain rose, the proscenium stage was bare except for an armchair, elaborately carved and upholstered in brocade.

Andrew strode out on stage in black tie. But, small and thin as he was, even the semi-formal wear couldn't endow him with any majestic presence. The poor soul came off like an apprentice waiter.

"Ladies and gentlemen," he projected to the back rows. "We thank you for coming to celebrate the ascension of our Sister, the Mystic Delphine, to the spirit plane. Tonight, you have been invited to meet Delphine's appointed successor and medium, the Mystic Sidney!"

"Oohs" and "ahs" greeted this concept, reverberating loudly through the auditorium.

Andrew held his left arm out in presentation, then backed into the right wing where he was, no doubt, immediately forgotten by all.

Now Sidney the beautician flounced across the stage, his avoirdupois straining at the seams of a royal blue jumpsuit and draped in a scarlet cape that flapped as he took his bows.

"Brothers and Sisters of the prophecy, I bring tidings!" he shouted, then ensconced himself in the armchair like Farouk on his throne. "The Mystic Delphine has chosen me as a medium to convey her message to you all, and she wishes me to assure her friends that she has come to a place of rest and peace."

Sidney closed his eyes, and then a transformation occurred. He sat up straighter in his chair and waved one hand gracefully, threw his head back, and brought his voice up nearly an octave.

"Good evening, my dear people."

I whispered, "That's Delphine's voice."

Julian spoke without moving his lips. "Or as close to it as any drag queen can get. I remember him flogging the same act back when he was emcee at the Powder Puff Review."

"During my lifetime, my dearest friend was Sidney Bowers," the Delphine impersonator continued. "And he has been generous enough to lend me his body for this evening. So I have been able to come back and speak with you again." The audience rumbled with exclamations: "Do you hear that?" "It really is her!" and "He's channeling her!"

Sidney held out a hand. "Does anyone here need guidance? Are there any questions?"

"Yeah, yeah!" a frizzy blond fairly screeched. "It's me, Jane Bittnah! Delphine, you remembah?" She climbed to her feet. "I *miss* you!"

"Thank you, Jane darling," Sidney intoned languidly. "I so miss you too."

"Now he sounds like Tallulah," Julian muttered.

"My question is . . . ," the woman went on, "I'm thinkin' 'bout buyin' anothah piece of proppity ona cawnah of Royal an' Desiah Streets. They's a key lot of three hunnet feet and a lotta space foh rental units. See?" Miss Jane held up a real estate photo of the 'proppity' under discussion and waved it so Delphine could make it out from her vantage point in Heaven. "On'y, the zonin' bawd don't wanna give me no variance t'add three moah appawtments."

Julian hissed, "Cripes. That's just two blocks from us."

"Yeah, just what we need, more population density," I whispered back. "I hope she burns in hell."

Miss Jane was just warming up. "Now I got this lawyah, Mistah Pete Goldman, who's on TV alla time. An' he tole me it'll cost me ten thousan' dollahs ta go ta cawt. Now, what I wanna know is . . . "

Julian held his hand over his mouth so as not to guffaw at the un-spiritual nature of Miss Jane's query.

I caught Sidney almost breaking character as he raised one eyelid a fraction to take measure of the querant. Real estate was not his area of expertise.

"If I can get interest at six pahcent"—Miss Jane held up a leaflet from a mortgage bank—"should I buy the proppity? Or, wait!" She dug into her purse for another real estate photo. "They's this othah place in Gretna, wheah I wouldn't need no variance, but I'd hafta get a new roof, which would cost six thousan' if my brothah does it."

"Yes, yes!" Sidney-Delphine-Tallulah broke in shrilly. "I understand your problem. There is someone close to you whose name starts with a *C.*"

"Uh-huh. That'd be my brothah Carl."

"Yes, yes! Carl is the one who has the answer. He will guide you to the right decision."

By now, Andrew had snuck around the back of the stage and rejoined the audience, where he acted as a shill, leading the applause from the right-hand aisle.

Other hands went up with questions, and Miss Jane was forced to yield her moment in the spotlight and resume her seat.

"But Carl don't know nutthin' 'bout real estate," she was grumbling under her breath. "He done dropped out ina nint' grade."

Sidney's put-on voice grew more strident.

"And now is there someone else who needs guidance?"

Julian groaned, "Saints preserve us. Now he's doing Bette Davis!"

"I *am* detecting a little bit of Margo Channing, now that you mention it. But I'm sure no one else has noticed."

"If he calls on someone named Peter, it's all over."

After another forty minutes of Sydney's improvisations, I left my seat, worked my way to the back of the hall, and slipped out into the lobby before the curtain fell. I picked up a copy of *Gambit* and made myself inconspicuous, for the purpose of reading the crowd.

"Wasn't he wonderful? I mean she," crooned a lovely young gum-chewer. "He knew everything about everyone who asked a question."

"It's so amazing," her Jeri-curled companion agreed. "The only mistake he made was with me. But maybe I'm just not sensitive enough."

"Don't feel pregnant. He didn't get anything about me right, either," the first girl said. "But I didn't want to spoil everything by contradicting him."

"Was he right about you in there?" a tall woman asked her taller, bearded escort.

"About my grandmother sending me a message from the spirit world? How could he be?" The man pulled out his key ring and rattled it. "Grandma's alive in Canarsie. She goes to the track every day."

"But you didn't call him on it?"

"Why embarrass the poor guy when everyone else is having so much fun? You wait here; I'll bring the car around."

I scuttled out to the sidewalk, where Julian was pacing in front of the steps. "What's the buzz?"

"His act wasn't very convincing, but nobody wanted to come right out and say it. The Emperor was pantless."

I took his arm to negotiate the cracked sidewalk on the way back to the parking lot.

"Holy cow! I just remembered tomorrow is Thanksgiving."

"What's the panic? The turkey is defrosting in the refrigerator even as we speak," Julian reassured me.

"Gaby is coming to eat it with us."

"As she does every year. So?"

"But this year, she's bringing a date, and we want to make a good impression."

"That lady has a *date*?"

"Why not? She's of age."

"She's *eighty*. Isn't that somewhat *past* the age?"

"Not really; Gaby's a Capricorn. Those people carry on forever. Since we're having guests, someone should clean the old place."

"Someone should," Julian agreed wholeheartedly as we reached the car.

"At least the living room, dining room, and kitchen. And one bathroom."

"One bathroom!" He unlocked my door and held it open. "Well, I'll certainly do my part. I'll unwrap the funny little soaps."

"Knock yourself out."

*M*y best friend, Gaby, has been a baroness in Zurich, a resistance fighter in Berlin, and a diplomat in New York. Now an octogenarian, her adventurous lifestyle has slowed down, at least to the point where she finds my company amusing.

She arrived for Thanksgiving dinner as elegant as always, her green velvet gown accessorized with a gold clutch bag, an emerald brooch, and a distinguished-looking gray-haired escort.

"Margo, dis iss Brad Duke, my new sveetheart."

"Happy Thanksgiving, Margo."

He handed me a bottle of white wine, a Meursault. I tried to read the vintage without my glasses.

"La Reine Pedauque, '87," he supplied.

"Neat label." I took his hat. "Your name is Duke? Hey, maybe you're descended from an actual Duke."

"Waal, it's more likely I'm descended from someone who *played* a Duke in a mummer's play back during the Middle Ages. You ever hear of a real duke named Duke?"

"Duke Duke? No." I hefted the bottle. "This will go just right with the dinner. My husband has drinks and cigars in the kitchen."

"Sounds good to me," Brad replied in a soft drawl, and followed the aroma of turkey roasting.

I pulled Gaby aside. "He's very charming; who is he?"

"Chust a nize retired engineer from Vest Virginia. Isn't he handsome?

"Yes, but how old is he?"

"Mickey Mouse and Brad chust had a birthday." She reached up and took out her hat pins. "Dey are both sixty-five."

"Why that's barely old enough for social security. Shame on you." I wagged my finger. "Why don't you go out with a man your own age?"

She lifted her hat off, stuck the pins back in, and clapped it on the hall rack.

"I vould haf to dig him up!"

Julian was in the kitchen tending the roast and regaling Brad with a bit of his crack.

"So, this tycoon comes up to me and says, 'I'll give you a million dollars to sleep with your wife.' So *I* say, 'But certainly! When and where do you want her?' "

"Mmm hmm." Brad was rummaging for a corkscrew.

"Then he has the nerve to stand there and tell me, 'No you don't understand. *You* have to sleep with her for the million.' Well, you can bet I just hauled off and punched that bastard right in the nose! I mean, after all, a man has his principles!"

"You see?" I intervened. "We've enjoyed an idyllic marriage for eighteen years." I put my arm around Julian's waist. "We'd never break the mood with that hot, messy foolishness."

Brad stood over his wine bottle, twisting the corkscrew expertly. "Speaking strictly for myself, I *like* to get messy and foolish."

Gaby took a stem glass. "I also. Oh, Margo, vee vent to see dat film."

"How was it?" Julian was basting. "I heard he had an Irishman playing a German and an Anglo-Indian playing a Jew."

"Und dey ver marvelous. It vas very authentic for da time. I almost felt dat I vas back der."

"You must have had friends who were caught up in that."

"Too many." Gaby held out her glass, and Brad poured her some wine. "Dey ver all assimilated you see. Dey thought dey ver goot Germans. I told my friend, 'Sophie, I vould not stay in dis country one minute! Chust take your jewelry in a little bundle and *go!* But she vas looking around at her grand house on Kurfürstendamm. 'But I can't leave my home. No, dis madman can't last.' Der vas no vay I could convince her. Of course, she vas transported."

Gaby shrugged slightly, the story being fifty years old for her.

I toddled to the refrigerator for a Coke. "Looking back in the context of the times, it seems she was foolish. But I understand her attitude. If someone told me the government was going to kill all the Irish-Americans and I had to flee the country with nothing but what I could carry, and start all over in some land where I don't even speak the language, *I* wouldn't believe them."

Julian closed the oven door. "Your people had their turn during the Potato Famine."

"Actually, it was not a famine but deliberate starvation," I corrected. "The land was producing quite enough to feed all the people on it, but it was under the control of the British landowners. So they shipped all the produce home to England and let us starve."

" 'Us'?" Brad turned his head. "You sound as though it were personal."

"It was, several times removed. I'm remembering the stories of my great-grandmother, Granny Armaugh. She never got over her hatred of the British. Wait, I'll show you her picture."

I sprinted into the living room and fetched the framed photograph of my eighty-two-year-old great-grandma in her old-fashioned, high-necked dress, holding a four-year-old girl with pigtails. I remember that I had been dressed for mass when the picture was taken.

I stopped to gaze at the faded image a moment. Granny Armaugh. She loved to braid my hair, she said, because it was the same red-gold her own had been. Her voice was so soft, it seemed not even to reach my ears, but I understood every word.

"Ye'll have to larn ta do this all by yerself, me darlin'. Soon Oi'll be goin' up t'Heaven ta be with Jaysus."

I said, "No, Granny. I don't want you to leave me."

"Sure an' Oi won't be leayvin' ye a'tall. Oi'll always be watchin' ye from me own wee cloud up above."

I remember that I started to cry then. "But you'll be so far away. Why do you have to go?"

"That's me reward fer bayin' good. When Oi'm in Heaven, Oi'll be able ta sing all day."

"You can sing all day here."

"Only fer you, my little love."

And then she would sing a lilting verse:

> *"Má faimse slante, is fada a beas tract ir,*
> *an meid is bathu i Anachcuain.*
> *Mo trua amaireac, gach athair is maithir,*
> *bean is paiste ata ag sileath deor."*

I understood the words when I was little, something about twenty-one people who drowned on their way to the county fair.

Granny Armaugh died three months after the picture was taken.

With appropriate ceremony, Julian carried the turkey to the table, and I began the surgery, holding out the drumsticks with the meat fork and cutting through the joints.

"It's a good night to entertain. There's nothing on television except the dozenth Kennedy special."

"It's the thirtieth anniversary," Brad said, breaking his corn bread. "Dallas was thirty years ago. I remember I was working in a plant in Wheeling when the news came out over the loudspeaker."

"That's one moment in time universally remembered." I put a chunk of white meat on Gaby's plate and asked, "What were you doing when you heard?"

"I vas having a late lunch with da Swiss consul, und da captain came to every table. Vee could not finish. Herr Lutoff had to hurry back to da embassy."

"I was in high school," Julian recalled. "Brother Clement's history class, ironically enough. Brother Booth came in and whispered to Brother Clement; then he made the announcement. While we kids sat there semiparalyzed, Brother Booth pushed on to the next class room and Brother Clement led us all through the Lord's Prayer. Who told you, Margo?"

The whole table turned politely to hear my story.

"A bellboy at the Plaza Hotel."

"What were you doing at the . . . ?" Julian squinched his eyes shut. "No. Please don't tell me."

The room descended into a prudent silence for a few minutes of cutting and chewing before Brad came up with a topic more fit for discussion.

"So what do y'all think?" he challenged the table. "You believe Oswald acted alone?"

"Not a chance," I said. "It was Carlos Marcello behind the whole operation."

"Castro," Gaby asserted.

"KGB," Julian speared a drumstick.

"But," I pointed out, "Oswald had known ties to the Mafia."

"He had ties to Cuba too," Gaby said.

"He certainly had ties to Russia."

Brad reached for the butter. "Poor fella had more ties than Betty Page."

I poured gravy on my meat. "After Ruby shot Oswald dead in front of all Television Land, I remember Johnny Carson had a joke: 'What happened to the elephant who walked into the Dallas Police Station?' And the answer was, 'Nothing. Nobody saw him.' "

Julian took a scoop of mashed potatoes. "Margo has been getting most of her hard news from the trash journalism shows."

"That's real life. *A Current Affair* devoted all last week to the enduring love affair between Joey and Mary Jo Buttafuoco."

"The 'Fun Couple' of the hour," Brad observed dourly.

"Now that Jim and Tammy Faye have split up, Burt and Loni have split up, they're the only couple left. They showed clips of their MTV music video, featuring Joey's snakeskin books and an Amy Fisher lookalike."

Julian raised an eyebrow.

"Good taste in the Long Island tradition."

"Well, it was a heartwarming send-off," I said. "After all, the romantic lead is about to spend six months in the slam for porking a teenager."

"He's lucky they use numbers instead of names in prison," Brad drawled. "That's the last place a man'd want to call himself 'Buttafuoco.'"

"He couldn't help himself," I said. "It's that uncontrollable animal sex drive. When I was young, I thought all men wanted to do it. And I thought half of them wanted to do it with *me*."

"That might have been true. When you were *young*."

"When I was and they were. But now we're not."

"I remember you had one dat was all man," Gaby put in. "Vat about your famous reformed gangster, Rocco Fortunado?"

"That gum has already been chewed."

Fourteen months ago, Rocco traded me in for a twenty-year-old, blond aerobics instructor.

There's a saying, "I don't care if he loves me and leaves me, so long as he leaves me enough." And Rocco left me much the richer for the association, so no hard feelings.

Last I heard, Rocco was keeping a silicon-augmented brunette cocktail waitress. He still takes me out to dinner sometimes when he craves adult conversation. On the order of, "My bimbo doesn't understand me."

Gaby took some stuffing. "Der vas some French man you ver interested in."

"Bernard."

"Yes, dats da name. Vasn't he rich und handsome enough for you?"

"Rather. And he was romantic and attentive too. Bernard employed the correct courtship technique—"

"Meaning he spent buckets," Julian elucidated.

"So on our fourth date, I let him know—subtly, of course—that I was ready to get intimate."

"By 'subtly' she probably means she grabbed his nethers," Julian said in an aside, which I ignored.

81

"Naturally, Bernard expressed appropriate joy and gratitude. But then he explained that the only part of a woman he considers erotic are the feet."

"The feet?"

"So, I said, 'That's no problem, mine are size nine. I'm *your* Dolly Parton!'"

"No lie." Julian pointed. "Look at those gunboats."

"I thought it would be no problem if the guy was turned on by feet."

"It's amazing the accommodations Margo will make for a man who's jingling some change."

"I'm very flexible, you know." I held my hands up behind my ears and flapped them. "I can hoist them right up there."

Julian grimaced. "So in her pathetic if never-flagging effort to please, our femme fatale sashayed out of the man's bathroom wearing nothing but shoes and socks."

"Lovely pink socks," I added. "And I seductively let him take them off, you know? But I soon found out that Bernard didn't want to play with my feet before sex, or after sex, or even *during* sex. But *instead* of sex!"

Julian picked up the fluted serving spoon. "The relationship was not all Margo hoped it would be."

"A girl likes being made love to above the ankles *once* in a while . . . Besides I'm ticklish."

Julian said, "So she sent the poor wretched pervert on his way and saved herself a fortune on pedicures."

"I should have known that any guy who was past fifty and still had a full head of hair wasn't going to be virile."

"Your husband still has a full head of hair," Gaby pointed out. "Isn't he virile?"

"How should I know?"

"It isn't that kind of marriage," Julian offered. "We're only staying together for the dog."

He leaned across the table. "Take some gravy. Don't be shy—Margo expects to enter that rarified club of hard journalists. She's investigating the unforeseen demise of the see-all, know-all Madame Delphine."

82

Gaby, who has never believed in anything and whose expression is one of permanent incredulity, twirled her teaspoon.

"Ach! Dat vas all fraud."

Brad was ladling on the rusty gravy. "Then how did she convince thousands of people she could foretell the future?"

"Any form of divination is pretty much a Rorschach test," I admitted. "I'll show you. Julian, my tarot deck is on the buffet behind you."

He passed it across, and I fanned the deck on the tablecloth beside my plate, ran my hand over the backs of the cards, drew one out, and held it up. "This is the Empress. What does she mean to you? She might look like your mother or your best friend. So then when you happen to get a phone call from your mother, or run into your best friend, you think you've experienced precognition." I gathered the cards together and slid them back in their box. "It's all subjective."

"Den vhy do so many people take it seriously?"

"We all want a little magic in our lives, don't we?"

Julian said, "David Ariane was working on the story too. But he's been taken off hard journalism for a while."

I suppressed a smirk. "Seems he made the whole station look stupid by running a news piece about a resurrected fly."

"I hear ringing." Julian raised his hand. "It's time to ignore the phone."

"But who would call on Thanksgiving?" I jumped up, hurried into the living room and flipped the light on to look at the caller ID number. "I can't ignore this one, gang. It's Frank Washington." I picked up on the fourth ring.

"How's your turkey?"

"I'll never know. Margo, I wanted to tell you this before you heard it on the television."

"Tell me what?"

"It's Sidney Bowers. They just found him in his apartment."

"Doing what?"

"Cooling down. He's been stabbed to death."

Sidney had thoughtlessly got himself murdered in his Dumaine Street apartment. I hated having to go down to the Quarter. It's only a ten-minute drive, but I needed at least another half hour to find a parking garage with space, hand my key to the valet, and totter along the cracked banquette to the seven hundred block of Dumaine. So it was nearly eight-thirty before I made it to the crime scene, where the coroner's wagon was just pulling away. Again, I had been deprived of the main exhibit. I spotted Duffy peering out the doorway and climbed over the yellow ribbon to reach him.

"Hey there! Frank called me. Where is he?"

Duffy thumbed the hallway behind him. "Right inside. He's interviewing the closest thing we have to a witness."

I got on my tiptoes and looked over his shoulder.

"Him? Bless us and save us."

"The closest thing to a witness" was a Generation Xer clad in black leather from neck to toe, sporting five rings in his ears and two in his nose.

"I don't know much," he was mumbling.

"Anyone can see that, Mr. Price," Frank said patiently. "But please, just tell us what you *do* know about the visitor."

"I can give you the time, um . . . " Price swayed to some band playing an exclusive engagement inside his shaven head.

"It had to be after twelve-thirty last night because we had just finished watching *Conan*. Then Gerald came up with his collar and leash and begged me to take him for a walk."

"Gerald is your dog?"

"My lover."

"Oh."

"Well, the door to the next apartment closed, and I saw the back of someone who was wearing a trench coat. I remember thinking it was strange because I knew Sidney lived alone. But the person was walking very fast."

"Was it a man or a woman?"

"I couldn't even tell that. Anyone can wear a trench coat."

Frank tapped his pencil. "Maybe Gerald saw something."

"I don't think so," Mr. Price addressed his boots. "You see, he . . . uh . . . was on all fours."

"I see."

"Was the cat in the trench coat black or white?" I interjected.

Frank frowned but then let the question hang in the air till Price answered with one word.

"White."

"How did you know? Did you see his hands or neck?"

"No, but . . . I remembered that I was a little curious, you know?"

"Yes. So?"

"If he was black, I would've been scared."

"Lieutenant?" Duffy waved a hand in a plastic glove. "Here's something you'll want to look at."

I clasped my hands behind my back to make it obvious that I wasn't touching anything and watched Frank pull on a plastic glove of his own and hold the proffered object. "It's an envelope addressed to Sidney. Postmarked three days ago, Central Post Office."

"What else?" Duffy teased.

"The most common twenty-nine-cent stamp, the kind that's vended in booklets . . . no return address. So what?"

" 'What' is the letter that came inside! Lookee here!" Duffy held a sheet of paper by the top, and it unfolded.

Frank read aloud: " 'You're the next phony psychic who goes down.' No signature, just that *P* with the extra stroke we found up in Lakeview."

"Pluto," I interjected.

"Exactly." Duffy grinned while slipping the letter into a glassine bag. "Did you note that it's written with the same typeface as on the envelope."

"So noted. The real puzzle is, why didn't Bowers tell the police he had been threatened?"

"He didn't take it seriously," Duffy suggested.

I cupped my hand around my ear. My cool ear feels good to my warm hand and vice versa.

"One phony psychic of his acquaintance had already been murdered, but he didn't take it seriously? Sidney didn't look like the brave type to me."

"Me neither."

*J*ulian pulled his hand away. "OK, that's enough, Catherine." She scrambled around to the other side of his chair and began pushing her nose under his left hand. He glanced down absently. "Well, what do you know? Another dog! I guess I'll have to pet this one too."

"It's only fair," I said, and winked at Catherine.

She wiggled and wagged at the attention. Coming from a different direction to get an extra petting was her oldest trick, and it still worked.

I walked to the window and pulled the draperies apart.

"I was feeling sorry for poor Sidney."

"Hmm?" He was busy petting. "Everyone goes sometime."

"But November is such a terrible month to die, don't you think?" I looked out the window. The street was just getting dark, with only a gray haze on the western horizon where the sun should be. "I mean, winter's on the way, and it's so cold and bare outside. And the worst part is . . ." The scene being that depressing, I closed the drapes. "You just miss the Christmas season."

"All the hassle."

"All the fun of shopping and putting presents under the tree, and the carols and the eggnog, and shortbread cookies and counting down to midnight on New Year's Eve. One last Christmas he should have had. That's what *I'd* want."

It was fresh from the printer. A full-color poster of the late Sidney Bowers in his cape, gazing off into the distance as though at a beautiful vision. THE MYSTIC SIDNEY SEES AND ANSWERS. At the bottom of the poster were blank spaces to fill in for the time and place of the seeing and answering.

"You know, I'd thought we actually had some kind of chance to retrieve the business." Andrew Berry slapped the desk. "We just might have pulled it out with Sidney's stage shows. But now . . . " He folded the poster and tore it into jagged pieces. "It's all a shambles. Somebody doesn't want the Delphine line in operation."

"Maybe. But it doesn't make sense that someone killed Sidney just to ruin your business."

"Why else? The police said the killer had threatened him because he was a 'phony psychic.' "

"But maybe that was just a distraction, see? It's more likely that Sidney was killed because he knew something."

Andrew screwed up his face. "What on earth could he know? He was a hairdresser."

"Delphine seemed to have pulled a lot of skeletons out of a lot of armoires over the years. Suppose she rattled some of them in front of her closest confidant?"

"That could have been the motive. But with both of them dead, it doesn't help us."

"It may just. Listen, Andrew, whatever Sidney knew, we can know too."

He took the seat directly across from me and focused intently.

"How?"

"It may have been connected with someone she met during any point in her life, so first I'll check into her background. Where she was born—"

"Cleveland," he interjected quickly. "That much I know."

"Good. Then we can start with Cleveland and just go through her life year by year, homes, schools, jobs, lovers . . . Eventually we could hit on whatever it was Sidney knew. That one person she identified with Pluto."

He was nodding. "That's a great idea, if the answer is in the past. But what if . . . ?" He squeezed his eyes shut. "No. I can't think about it."

I took up the thought. "But what if Delphine and Sidney really were killed just because they were phony psychics?"

*W*hile I was waiting in the Royal Street courtyard, I ordered a latte, only because it was the closest thing they had to real food. (Like a chocolate malt.)

I was already slurping the bottom of the glass when my contact sauntered in, camouflaged in a wide-brimmed hat and sunglasses. She took the chair beside me and whispered, "You have it?"

"Here it is." I passed her Delphine's phone directory, wrapped in this week's *Gambit*.

"Good." She held the *Gambit* over her open purse and let the directory slip down into it. "I've got something else you might like."

After wriggling around a moment, she pointed to her lap.

Discreetly (I pray) I glanced down, then had to bend over and focus. "It's a check. Delphine's?"

She nodded vigorously. "Look who it's to."

I squinted. "Randall Jooby. But what for?"

"Dunno. She never told me. But one afternoon, she asked me to get in my car and follow him. Find out where he kept his important stuff."

"Were you able to do that?"

"I think so. He went right to the Black Hat Club, where they have all those magic shows. The box office lady told me Jooby has a little office of his own behind the stage. But I couldn't go in there."

"No, you couldn't," I agreed.

"So Delphine never mentioned him again. But I found this check with the bank statement. It's dated the day after I followed Jooby to the Black Hat Club."

"That's some great work. It should be worth another hundred." I pulled out my wallet.

She pulled down her dark glasses and winked. "I made you a photocopy. Both sides."

"You're very efficient, Didi."

"I'm Nona."

I stood on the corner of Royal and Governor Nicholls, wondering whether to take a cab, which would cost six bucks with tip; phone Julian to pick me up; or try to hobble twenty-one blocks in heels.

While I was deliberating on the problem, a big black sedan stopped in front of me, and a handsome thirty something with a strong classic jaw sprung out of it and joined me on the sidewalk.

"Aren't you Mrs. Fortier?"

"Yes," I beamed, glad to be someone he was interested in.

He bowed like a royal emissary. "Lieutenant Washington sent me to pick you up."

"He did?"

His carriage was a sumptuous Cadillac with dark tinted windows so the peasants outside couldn't see the aristocrats riding in state within. He opened the door of the passenger's side, and the black leather seat beckoned from within the plush interior.

My feet will usually go as long as four hours in Easy Spirit shoes, but their time was up now and they were starting to hurt so much that I just sighed in appreciation. The man took my moment of silent gratitude for hesitation.

"Don't worry," he smiled. "You can trust me."

Trust? The word reverberated through my brain. "Niver . . . niver . . . niver . . . "

"Of course." I returned his smile and raised it by four teeth. "I've just got to tell Officer Duffy . . . Hey, Sid?" I reeled around and shouted at an imaginary Officer Duffy, just out of sight around the laundromat building. "Come on! Frank sent a car for us!"

I hadn't quite finished the thought before the handsome guy was back in his Cadillac and gunning the engine toward Esplanade. I tried to see the license plate, but the number had been obscured by a careful application of red clay.

I decided to take a cab.

"Sounds like Hubie Nadler. What do you think?"

Frank turned to his computer and clicked an icon.

Duffy leaned over his shoulder. "Absolutely."

I opened my purse and rummaged for my pad. "Who's Hubie Nadler?"

"He's a freelance hitman who works out of his car—rather *in* his car. Nadler's got himself a rolling abattoir with tinted windows."

"So no one can see the victim inside, pounding on the glass." Duffy mimed the desperate pounding.

"There will be a handle on the inside of the passenger's door, but it will be a dummy. You can't open it, see?"

"I'm confident in saying that if you had entered Nadler's car, you never would have been heard from again." Frank shivered. "Of course, we've never been able to prove any of this to a jury's satisfaction because there have been no living witnesses to the crimes themselves."

Duffy nodded. "We got all our info from jailhouse snitches. Nadler's talent is that he can make himself absolutely harmless-looking, like the boy you'd want your daughter to marry. Say, what tipped you off about the creep?"

"He asked me to trust him."

"I wish you could say he tried to pull you into the car." Frank looked at me sideways. "That's what I wish."

"I wish I could too. But there were people around."

A large woman in uniform carried in a file and dropped it on his desk without a word. Frank withdrew a photo of a weak-chinned nerd with thinning blond hair and pushed it across the desk.

"Recognize it?"

"No, I've never seen him before."

Duffy shook his head. "Too bad."

Frank frowned. "Look again, Margo. That's Hubie Nadler, the fellow who so generously offered you a ride to oblivion."

I picked up the photo. "It can't be. The man I saw was handsome, with a much stronger jaw. And I remember he had a widow's peak."

Frank slapped the table. "See? We'll never get the scumbag."

"Yeah?" Duffy chortled. "So he was handsome this time?"

"This time?"

"He's a master of disguise," Frank explained. "The jaw was a prosthetic, the widow's peak a toupee. Sometimes he wears a false mustache or beard."

"But very realistic looking," Duffy said. "Then there's the colored contacts, cheek pads, nose plugs . . . "

"He's a quick-change artist. The point is that in two minutes he can rip off, wipe away, and spit out the whole mess; shove it in his briefcase; and walk right past any bystanders, who won't even recognize him the second time they see him."

"I can identify the creep," I persisted. "All he'd have to do is put on the same disguise he was wearing when I saw him."

"Wouldn't any defense attorney love that?" Frank smirked. "A suspect is required to make himself up to look like a felon."

"I'm for it." Duffy clapped his hands. "We'd get a hundred percent case clearance."

"Anyway, that's all the hint I need, Margo. You're in mortal danger of following your friends, Delphine and Sidney, into the great beyond."

"I'll be careful."

"You can't be careful enough. I don't want you wandering the streets without a police officer." He pushed his intercom. "Is she in the building yet, Doris? Okay, send her in."

Two minutes later, I was looking at a uniformed policewoman, barely over five feet tall but tough looking.

"This is Officer Marilou Gendron."

"Officer Gendron? I heard she's the most decorated woman on the force? You mean you're assigning her to *me*?"

"Don't flatter yourself. I'm assigning *you* to *her.* Officer Gendron is one of my best people. I can't spare her from her normal duties."

"So what will I do?"

"So you will, in your capacity as a journalist, accompany Officer Gendron on a ride-along throughout her usual shift."

Duffy nudged him. "Don't forget, she has to sign a waiver."

I drew back. "What kind of waiver?"

Frank dug into his drawer. "A simple one absolving the police department and the city of New Orleans from any liability."

"You mean in case someone tries to shoot Officer Gendron and misses and blows my fool head off instead?"

A grin. "Exactly. Here it is. By the *X* please."

The radio crackled: "We've got a Domestic at eighteen-forty Herbert Street. You're familiar with that one, Officer."

"On my way."

She reached under the seat and pulled out three large-size trash bags, neatly folded. "You get to carry these."

"What for?"

"You'll see."

Eighteen-forty Herbert was the right half of a shotgun double and quite audibly the scene of a domestic disturbance. We could hear the growls and the blows and the screams even out on the sidewalk.

A motherly looking woman stood in front of the building, wringing her hands.

"Oh, Officer! I had to call you. He's beating on her again. I'm afraid he's killing the girl this time."

Marilou kept her hand on her holster as she ascended the stoop and knocked on the paint-flecked door.

"Police! Open up!"

I followed at a discreet distance, with my commission of garbage bags.

The door was jerked open in such a way as to loosen its hinges, and an angry, red-faced drunk glowered down at us.

"Whadaya want?!"

"We've met before, Mr. Callahan. You know what I want. Step aside, please." The hand stayed on the holster. Callahan moved away from the door, and Marilou walked in as though she were about to take over the joint. I stepped in after her, clutching the plastic bags to my bosom.

"Jus' a little argument with my wife. Nobody's business."

Behind him cringed the wife, a pale, thin half-person, eyes and nose wet. She moved along the wall like a mouse.

I thought the argument might have been about laundry, as pieces of wadded-up clothing were littered all over the room.

Marilou deftly sidestepped the mess.

"Are you ready to press charges, ma'am?"

"No ... I ... I ... " The lady of the house swallowed hard and tried again. "I just want to get away from him."

"Fuckin' shit!" Callahan's eyes bugged out. "She's not goin' anywhere!"

"She's coming with us," the sergeant said. "Get your things together, ma'am."

The mouse bent and began picking up skirts and dresses.

"Okay, that's what she wants? Sure she can get out right now!" The husband's face was red, and his nose looked inflated. "But she's not taking any of those clothes!"

Marilou put her hands on her hips. "Are you a transvestite, sir?"

"What!" The nose grew yet redder. "Of course not!"

"Then we can assume, can't we, that any female attire in this house belongs to *Mrs.* Callahan."

"But I bought it!"

"For her?"

"Yes!"

"Then it's hers."

That piece of logic stumped him for a moment, but then the mouse started sobbing. "I ... I don't need the clothes. Just let him have them."

"No, ma'am. I'm not leaving him anything to hold over you or any reason for you to return. Margo?"

So that was what the bags were for. I stooped and set to work picking up the woman's wardrobe, a collection of rags not even good enough for a garage sale, and stuffing it into a Hefty bag, grunting with the exertion on old bones. The mouse took another of the bags and joined me in my task, still sobbing, while Callahan snorted above us. The only person remaining silent was Officer Gendron, who guarded our backs as we carried our loads down the front steps.

We were out in the unit and halfway down the block before Mrs. Callahan spoke again. A whimpered, "I have no place to go."

Obviously, I thought. If she'd had any folks of her own, she wouldn't have stayed with that neanderthal.

Officer Gendron turned left on Canal and spoke into her radio. "Notify Toby Castle that I'm on my way with another guest." Someone answered with a crackle, and she hung up.

"A guest?" the mouse whimpered.

"Don't worry, I'm taking you to the Domestic Aid Center. You can stay there until you make other arrangements."

"Domestic Aid?"

"It's a battered women's shelter," I blurted, then Mrs. Callahan gripped the seat back with both hands, the sergeant gave me a look, and I zipped it up. Battered women aren't willing to be categorized as battered women.

The redoubtable Elizabeth, all two hundred and fifty pounds of her, awaited us at the gate of the Domestic Aid Center. Elizabeth didn't trouble to introduce herself but simply hefted the mouse's bags of belongings as easily as though they were filled with air and waved a "follow me" signal.

Mrs. Callahan, now meeting someone at least twice as macho as her husband, fell into step and followed the leader into the house without looking back.

"I have some hope for this one." Marilou looked in her rearview mirror and backed the big Ford LTD out of the cramped parking spot, in an easier maneuver than I can make with a broom. "She looks like she never had anything."

"Why would that encourage you?"

"Trailer park trash may be the most adaptable. A job flipping burgers would support their customary lifestyle, so they know they can go anywhere. The worst candidates for rescue are those middle-class home-makers. Mrs. Brick House gets pulverized by her husband for the tenth time, and she's ready to run anywhere *except* to her own family."

"Why not her own family?"

"Because her nice, respectable, middle-class parents are dead sure to ask . . . " Here she affected a prissy, nasal, "middle-class" accent. " 'But, dear! Whatever did you do to set him off like that? We know he wouldn't have beat you up without a good reason. Now go right home, and try to be a better wife.' "

We turned left on North Claiborne and passed under the overpass as Marilou continued with her discourse. "She can't bring herself to tell any-one about her 'shame.' And neither can she risk the abusive husband finding her again. So now the woman is nameless, cut off from friends, family, and income."

"She can get herself a job."

"Right." Marilou had now assumed a singsong monotone. She had given this recitation before. "So she decides to get herself a job and tries to find something in the classifieds. Then it doesn't take the woman long to realize that her liberal arts degree isn't worth spit in the job market and that she's not qualified for anything that pays better than five dol-lars an hour." The sergeant twisted the steering wheel, and we headed down a side street. "Now, how is she going to rent an apartment, sup-port her kids, and pay for full-time childcare?"

"How *is* she?"

"She's not. People who are used to welfare have developed resources. They have cheap housing, jobs off the books, relatives to watch the ba-bies. But not Mrs. Respectable."

"Alimony?"

"What?" She threw her head back and laughed. "Where did you get *that* word? The husband will have their bank account cleaned out and all the assets in his brother's name before wifey can even mop up her tears. He'll quit his job, let his business go bankrupt, and swear in court that he's indigent. He would rather put everything they own in a pile and burn it than give her a cent."

The car swerved around a kids' game of basketball. I held on to the shoulder harness.

"Come to think of it, every recently divorced man I ever met claimed he was broke."

"Exactly. So now the newly liberated wife is stuck in the Domestic Aid Center, sharing a room with her kids, maybe even bunking with another miserable woman and *her* set of kids."

"It is sort of crowded and noisy in that place."

"So before long, she gets to thinking about that nice quiet spacious house back in Metairie, with her own bedroom, her own backyard, her own side-by-side washer and dryer. And she knows she'll never be able to buy those things for herself. She wants back what she had. So dear husband starts to look sweeter from a distance."

"And she's willing to believe him when he says he'll never hurt her again."

"She has to believe him. It's a matter of survival." The sergeant shook her head, and her shiny brown hair swung. "What can I do? I can't take them all home and support them."

"What did you think of that creep trying to hold onto his wife's *clothes*?"

"Standard procedure, Margo. No doubt he figures she'll be desperate enough to go back to get them."

"Did you ever notice, when a woman leaves a guy, he tries to take back everything he ever gave her."

"Does that surprise you?"

"It isn't reasonable. If I quit my job at the paper, my boss wouldn't try to take back all the wages I had earned over the years."

"A man likes to believe he *gives* a woman things, not that she's earned them."

"And what he giveth, he can taketh away."

"Exactly. It's all about power." Marilou picked up the radio, said some numbers into it, then got back to me.

"There was this woman I knew, Lydia. Her husband got drunk and slapped her a few times, but she didn't think it was too bad. She didn't want to leave him, because he was making good money, and every time he sobered up, he said he was really sorry and he'd give her a piece of jewelry."

"Typical."

97

"But it got worse, month by month, every time he got drunk. I, my-self, took her to the hospital twice, but she would never press charges. She claimed she had a plan. So one Saturday night the creep had his usual load on and he hit her as usual, but this time, Lydia hollered, 'One!' He didn't even notice but went and hit her again, and she hollered, 'Two!' Now he noticed, and he got even madder, so he hit her again and she yelled, 'Three!' It went on like that until 'Twenty-nine!' and he was too tired even to hit her again, so he just staggered off to bed."

"That's frightening," I said, to say something.

"Then when the creep woke up, he was shackled to the bed, hand and foot, and Lydia was standing over him with a tire iron." Marilou grinned. "She clubbed him over the knee and yelled, 'One!' Then across the belly, 'Two!' She kept right on going, all the way up to twenty-nine. Broke his arms, his legs, his feet . . . I don't know how she found enough space on the creep to hit him all those times without landing on a vital spot."

"Wasn't that sort of dangerous? I mean he was bound to take it per-sonally."

"Naturally, she'd had her suitcase all packed for days, with all her jew-elry and all the cash she could draw out of their joint accounts. She called his mother from the plane to take him to the hospital. You can do that now, you know. Make a phone call from up in a plane."

"So I've heard. What happened to the creep?"

"Now he walks on two canes. He hasn't been able to locate Lydia." Marilou chortled. "In New Zealand."

"I'm glad Lydia lived happily ever after."

"But she took a stupid chance. What if he'd crippled or killed her that last time? No, I don't approve. Besides, who could be happy in New Zealand?"

The radio crackled again in a higher pitch this time. "Scene of shoot-ing, thirteen-fifty Ruth Street." The shooting was clearly more urgent than a mere "Domestic."

"Someone shot through the front window of Duchess Theatrical Sup-plies. Barely missed the proprietor—"

"Ten-four. We're on our way."

Ours was the third unit on the scene and was quickly followed by two more. A tall, black officer introduced Marilou to the intended victim, one Murray Goldstein, who was still trembling at the fragility of his own mortality."

"If I hadn't moved that mirror . . . "

He clutched his Star of David pendant as though it were the magic talisman that had saved his life.

"I always keep the full-length mirror in front of that cupboard . . . ," he was jabbering. "But . . . but I needed some eyelashes so I moved it . . . I . . . "

A young patrolman handed the terrified storekeeper a plastic cup of water. He drank it down, then continued shakily.

"I moved it over behind the counter. There!"

He didn't have to point. The mirror, propped up behind the cash register, had become the focal point of the scene, due to its spider-webbed bullet hole some six inches from the top.

"I was standing right here, trying to remember where I put the new carton of spirit gum. I was facing the mirror, and I could see myself in it."

A blond in uniform stepped into the shop. "I checked it out from across the street. From the angle that Mr. Goldstein was reflected in the mirror, it would have looked like he was standing there in his usual place behind the cash register. The gunman aimed right at what he thought was the man's head."

"Anyone out there see anything?"

"Nothing. The store across the street has been vacant for six months. See, it's all boarded up." We all looked. It sure was. "The shooter broke in from the rear, pulled some crates over to the front door to stand on, and shot over the transom."

A black patrolman arose from behind the counter.

"The shot went straight through the mirror and hit the back wall."

I stayed to watch the forensics man dig around the bullet to extract it. He left a big ugly hole in the wainscotting, but the intended murder victim was too frightened to notice.

"If he'd come five minutes sooner, I would have b-been standing there instead of the mirror. And . . . And I'd be *dead*!"

Marilou asked, "Did you see who it was, Mr. Goldstein?"

"See? See?! If I had *seen* someone p-pointing a g-gun into this store, do you think I would have just *stood* here?"

"Is there anyone who would like to see you dead?"

"Yes, there is." Goldstein shook his fist over his head. "Julius Terwilliger. That's who."

A pen was uncapped. "Terwilliger?"

"Yes!" Goldstein raised his voice to a high pitch. "At Stagecraft Products on St. Charles Avenue."

"Did Mr. Terwilliger threaten you?"

"He certainly did. That queen claims I'm underselling him on pancake! But all I ever did was give a discount to regular customers who buy in bulk. God, *everyone* does *that*."

*I*t was late afternoon, and no show was in progress at the Black Hat Club, but the box office lady was on duty in her booth. I showed my press ID. "I'm Margo Fortier. I'll be doing a piece about the charity show this weekend."

"No one's in there yet. But you can go look around, if you want to."

I walked through the musty auditorium, climbed the steep steps to the stage, and tiptoed past the paraphernalia of the conjurer's art, a brightly figured cabinet with a dozen jigsawed holes and BOX OF DOOM painted in ten-inch Gothic letters, then a rack of vicious-looking scimitars that probably fitted precisely through those holes.

As Nona (or Didi) had said, there was a tiny office behind the back curtain, with a battered metal desk and a three-drawer filing cabinet. I rummaged through the files to *D* for *Delphine* and found nothing. But *H* for *Harris* had a manila folder with five pages of notes.

I was just closing the office door when I heard two voices at the side entrance, one discernible as Jooby's. I tried to push the pages into my purse, but they wouldn't fit and I didn't have time to run all the way across the stage into the orchestra. There was only one possible hiding place, the colorful but less than inviting Box of Doom. In seconds, I'd unlatched the little door, ducked down, and folded myself inside, with the notes clutched to my sagging bosom.

"It's all in the presentation, Jamsie," Jooby was saying as two sets of footsteps crossed the stage.

"I tried to follow your instructions," said a younger voice. "But, for some reason, the way I do it isn't going over."

"You work the illusion all right, but keep in mind that eighty percent of the show is showmanship. You need more razzle-dazzle to get the most out of this effect." I heard the metallic glide of a scimitar being slid out of its groove. "First the sword."

I heard it sing through the air.

"Now watch me. You have to make a big production of demonstrating that this is pure steel and sharp, to misdirect the audience. That way they don't stop to consider that it's the *box* that's rigged, see?"

"Right," agreed his audience of one.

"So you make a member of the audience authenticate the sword, preferably someone everybody knows so they won't think you're using a ringer. If Mayor Bartholemy is sitting out front, take it to Mayor Bartholemy. 'And Your Honor, would you please run your fingers along the blade and assure your constituents that it's genuine?' " I heard footsteps go to the lip of the stage and then return. "Thank you, Your Honor."

"I don't think people would trust the mayor these days," the acolyte mumbled.

"Then you continue to hold the sword over your head, like this, so no one can suspect a switch. Now to the box." His voice resounded in the empty theater. " 'And then as the beautiful young maiden awaits, helpless, within the chamber of doom . . .' That sadistic touch is part of the attraction."

"Yeah, I get it," the younger man grunted.

"The cold steel is applied!"

I put my eye up to one of the slits but then jerked aside without a second to spare as the scimitar came sliding through, right past my nose, and then out the corresponding slit at the opposite corner.

"You twist it a little on the way in, as though you've just encountered a fleshy thigh, so the audience thinks maybe you made a fatal mistake."

"You did that great. Like a master!"

102

"Naturally. Now *you* try one."

"Okay."

I heard the whoosh of another scimitar cutting the air and Jamsie's voice in imitation.

"Ladies and gentlemen, while the luscious damsel remains trapped inside, I place another sword through the chamber of doom, thus!"

I pulled back the fabric of my blouse with both hands, and the sword barely missed skewering it. I sucked my stomach in as the second blade came up through the bottom and out the top and cursed my large lunch.

"Now we turn the box around and around to demonstrate that it can't be attached to a secret trap door."

The two men did this with a will, turning my chamber of doom so fast that I was within seconds of losing that same large lunch. Then suddenly the turning stopped, and I hoped the crack of my head against the side of the box wasn't audible.

"Hello?" This came from a third voice. "I was supposed to meet my wife here. Margo Fortier. Has she come by?"

Thank my patron saint! It was Julian.

"No," Jooby said. "We haven't seen anyone."

"She's writing up the charity show in her column, and we have the owner's permission to look around."

I dared to peep through an unoccupied slit, to see that the two magicians' backs were to me. I stuck my pinky out of the slit and wriggled for all I was worth. Thank heaven I'd had a manicure. The flash of red must have caught Julian's eye. I saw him choke. But then he turned the choke into, "Hey!" and added, "This is one of your famous stage illusions, right?"

"One of them."

Jamesie wasn't showman enough to pretend he wasn't annoyed at the intrusion.

"Well, splendid." Julian said with all the élan of the born privileged. Then I felt him sit himself down right on top of my chamber of doom, which didn't help my natural claustrophobia. "I'm just going to hang around and watch. Maybe I can figure out how your trick works."

"Sorry, we never reveal our secrets to nonmagicians." I heard one scimitar slide against another as both were withdrawn from the box smoothly enough that they didn't make any detours through my hide along the way. "That's it for now, Jamesie. Good day, Mr. Fortier. I hope your wife shows up, safe and sound."

Then two sets of footsteps, one striding purposefully, the other scrambling, crossed the stage and became muffled behind the wing curtains.

After I'd stopped hearing them altogether, the little door to my prison opened and I looked up at Julian, shaking his head.

"When I realized you were stuck in there with those swords, I was scared out of my wits."

"Umph!" I had to roll out of the box in a curled lump. "You had reason to be scared."

Julian bent to help me straighten my limbs and hoisted me to a standing position.

"It's just that I happen to know you're not an identical twin."

I filled my lungs with blessed air, reeled around, and caught his shoulder. "See, this box is an illusion, painted to appear much smaller than it is. What looks like a platform *under* the box is actually part of the box itself and allows an extra foot of space inside." I knocked to demonstrate the hollow sound. "The magician's assistant is able to arrange her lithe young body in such a way that all the swords pass over, in front of, or behind her."

"But supposing the body inside the box is neither lithe nor young?"

"You can end up with a disgusting-looking shish kebab." I tried to massage a knot out of my leg. "But I'd rather have been skewered by every sword in Jooby's arsenal and be found sloppy dead in a pool of blood than let that pompous jerk know that I was crouching like a fool inside his tacky box." I held up the pages. "Look here."

"A clue?"

"Five pages of research Jooby did on Delphine's operation." I held one directly under the light and tilted my head back to read it without the aid of my trusty bifocals. "I've got to scan them real quick, then get them back to the filing cabinet. He learned the brand of microphone she used to eavesdrop on audience members. She'd be listening backstage while her eager fans chatted before the show."

Julian nodded, then struck a pose. "Oh, dearie me, Elsie," he falsettoed. "I'm going to ask Delphine about my diverticulitis. Do you think Dr. Schwartz is right about this prescription?"

I caught the ball. "Exactly. So later during the show, Delphine sings out, 'There's a dear lady in the rear of the house with diverticulitis. I see a professional man who is helping you with this. His name starts with an *S*. Does that mean anything to you?' "

" 'Ooh, *yes*," Julian replied, in the high-pitched cadence of the afflicted querent. "That would be Dr. Schwartz!"

I was still being Delphine. " 'And would you happen to have on your person a piece of paper that he gave you?' "

" 'My goodness, yes!' " Julian shrieked, in character. " 'This prescription right here in my purse! She's *amazing,* isn't she Elsie?' "

Something in the file caught my attention, and I closed the act. "This is funny. On the margin, he wrote 'Miss Rosen,' then a trail of dollar signs and a question mark."

"Miss Rosen?"

16

*T*he Star Restaurant on Decatur Street features live lobsters exhibited in a tank for selection by discerning patrons. I wasn't cold-hearted enough to designate the actual crustacean condemned to lose his quiet life for my dinner but let an anonymous one be cooked up and brought to the table.

"I'm just helping him to meet his karma," I said between bites. "If he was a good, virtuous lobster, he'll be reincarnated as a higher form of life, like a cow."

"So you can eat him again," Martin Koenig said.

"Exactly."

I dipped a piece of claw in the drawn butter. I always assume that the rule of calories will be suspended on special occasions, like when someone else is paying for my dinner.

Martin nodded over his surf-'n'-turf entrée and gazed around at the posters of long-departed movie stars adorning the walls. He pointed with his chin. "She was my favorite. Marilyn."

"The greatest," I admitted to my potato. "A total failure as a human being, but as a screen presence, she was luminous."

"Unparalleled in all of time and space."

"You think it was the Kennedys?"

"No way."

"Me neither. She didn't need any enemies. I studied her charts."

"So did I. She was meant to have children. Just think. If only that army photographer, David Conover, had never showed up at the Radioplane plant, she might have stayed with Jim Dougherty, had lots of kids, and lived out her life as a happy, fulfilled woman."

"But then *we* wouldn't have had her."

"No."

"How about you?" He leaned forward. "Were there any matinee idols in your fantasies?"

"Absolutely." I pointed over his shoulder. "Ray Milland, the most macho film actor ever."

"That limey fop? Come on. He was no John Wayne."

"You kidding? He made Wayne look like a pansy. Milland was a pilot, a steeplechase rider, and a marksman. He could ride better and shoot better than any other actor in Hollywood. Look it up."

"All that really impressed me about the guy is that he slept with Grace Kelly."

"She had all the luck, didn't she? I used to watch him on the *Late Show* kissing Wendy Barrie or Claudette Colbert and wish fervently that I'd been born twenty years earlier, just so I could have got it on with Ray Milland."

We ate in silence for a few minutes before Martin put his fork down and broached the main topic.

"I'd like to get it on with you."

"Really?"

It always comes to this, and I never know what to answer. How to address the issue of terms.

I finished chewing, then prefaced with, "Physically, you're very attractive."

"So are you. So what about it? Can we get together?"

"Martin"—I reached around the dinner plates and took his hand—"if all you want is sex, you can hire the most beautiful call girl in town, *and* her sister, for a fraction of what *I* would cost you."

"Duly noted." He kept my hand. "I don't want a call girl. Or her sister. But I do enjoy the company of a beautiful, intelligent woman my own age." He waved his napkin. "I know there are hundreds with those qualifications fluttering around town, but most of them are married or want to *get* married. And I'm not interested in that level of commitment. I'm used to living alone."

"I see."

"I also know your husband is homosexual and doesn't interfere with your personal life."

"I . . . uh . . . "

"And that suits me fine. Safely married, but not restricted."

"Hardly restricted." I put my green eyes on low beam. "But it's only fair to warn you that I would not be an economical mistress."

"I consider myself warned. He leaned over his empty lobster shells. "Do you have a specific amount in mind?"

"You remember what J. P. Morgan said about yachts?"

" 'If you have to ask how much, you can't afford it.' Yeah, that's what I heard. See, I've done some research. You and your husband together don't make enough money to support the lifestyle you like to describe in your column." He pointed his dessert fork. "That mink coat you're wearing is the most expensive accessory you've got, and Rocco Fortunado bought it for you."

Instinctively, I pulled the coat around me. "Why, I . . . "

(The mink was a kiss-off present.)

I assumed an expression of cool propriety.

"Rocco is a good friend."

"Right."

Martin took a forkful of mousse. "We belong to the same golf club, so I contacted him for a reference. Without giving out any details, Fortunado implied that you were worth the tariff."

"Indeed! He is a man of some means and generosity," I allowed.

"Yes, so am I. And at this time, I don't have anything better to do with my dough, and I think you'd be worth the expense. I could take you shopping to start things off, but the stores are closed tonight and I'm impatient, so . . . " He reached into his right jacket pocket and withdrew a rectangular box. "Here's a small token of my appreciation."

I accepted the token gracefully.

"A girl loves to be appreciated."

I opened the box and smiled so hard my ears rang. For therein nestled a string of pearls, at least eight millimeters each, perfectly matched for size and color so far as I could see. I picked them up and tried to read the clasp, but fat chance without my bifocals. I drew them across my teeth, and they felt slightly gritty. Real.

One hour and ten minutes later, I was wearing the pearls and nothing else.

The fact that Martin was a great lay was a bonus. I was so turned on that he could have just sprawled there like a carp and it wouldn't have dampened my enthusiasm. As a matter of policy, I agree with the late Sam Kinison, who advised that the best foreplay for a woman is "JEWELRY!"

Martin reached behind his headboard, and the Victorian chandelier above us brightened by maybe fifty lumens. Too many. I closed my eyes.

He said, "Margo, I've been holding back."

"No, you haven't." My voice was muffled in the crisp linen sheet. "Not one inch."

"I don't mean that way." He sat up, and I heard him fold his pillow for use as a backrest. "I told you I joined the psychic line to do horary research. But that was only part of it. I had a second, more important, agenda."

"Umph." I didn't open my eyes. "Unh?"

"It was about Harriet Rosen."

Now I came alert and propped up on my elbows. "Harriet Rosen?" This was the third time I'd heard the name.

"Delphine and her gang of thieves bilked her out of most of her money by staging phony séances."

I levered up to a sitting position. "So I heard." All of a sudden modest, I wrapped the top sheet around my sagging nudity. "Dan Aparisi told me about the scam. But he said there was no plausible complainant. Miss Rosen was supposed to be a spinster with no children."

"That's true." Martin frowned. "I was only a nephew, and she had no other close relatives. In the year before she died, I had been dividing my time between New York and Hong Kong. I'd phone every couple of weeks, and she'd just say she was fine and tell me about the latest events on *Guiding Light.* So I didn't worry about her." He shook his head. "I blame myself that I wasn't there at the end."

"You didn't guess anything was wrong."

"Not until afterward. I flew down for the funeral and set about clearing up her estate. That's when my aunt's lawyer told me all the assets had been liquidated in the months before she died. I had to know why." His voice was calm, as though delivering a stock report. "I went through all her cancelled checks for the previous two years. She had donated one-point-six million to Delphine's Psychic Research Center. I had to ask myself, what for?"

"She was a believer."

"Apparently." He snorted. "I didn't really need Aunt Harriet's money, but I didn't like the idea of losing my inheritance to a con artist, either." He shifted to the edge of the bed, pulled a cigar out of his humidor, and rolled it between his fingers. "Aunt Harriet had full control of her mental faculties and had the right to do whatever she liked with her own assets, so the police didn't have any interest in the case as it stood. That left me the single option of going to work for Delphine. I figured I could get inside the operation and learn enough to implicate her on a felony charge."

"And did you?"

"No such luck. I already told you, she stayed away from the psychics, figuring they'd read her for the phony she was, so I didn't see her around much. One day when Delphine was out shopping, I went sneaking around the house to look for evidence. Did you get a load of her office?" He picked up an ashtray. "The place was done over in pink, top to bottom. It looked like the inside of a snatch."

"Did you get into her files?"

"I never had access to the pertinent ones. I think Andrew kept them in his own apartment down in the Quarter." Martin picked up a little clipper and snipped the end off his cigar. "Then I faced the fact that I'm a bad detective. But . . . " He chuckled. "Fortunately, I'm a *rich,* bad detective. So I made the drop."

"The drop?"

"I'd found the one man in the operation who, without being an insider, knew everything that was going on inside."

"And that was . . . ?"

"Sidney. I paid him ten grand to tell me what he knew."

"Ten gee's?" I whistled low. "That would make *me* talk like a room-ful of mynah birds."

"As did he. Under that incentive, Sidney told me how Delphine had tricked my aunt out of nearly all her fortune by hiring an actress to play her mother's ghost."

"So you knew about the scam before Delphine died."

"Two weeks before. I didn't tell you right away, because I thought you were some kind of investigative reporter."

"But I *am*."

"Yeah, sure." He struck a kitchen match by flicking it with his thumb-nail, let the sulfur burn off, then applied the flame to his cigar. "So I was about to hire professional investigators to get the evidence I couldn't find. Maybe a private eye to trace down her contacts. Maybe a computer hacker to raid her files."

"What would that get you? The police can't act on illegally obtained evidence."

"I confess that I was going to worry about the legal technicalities later. Then I was going to sue her to recover the monies. But now she's out of my reach." He took three short puffs on his cigar and watched the smoke drift up around the chandelier. "Now that it's all out, I hope you're not mad at me for holding back."

I twisted around and reached for my underthings.

"There's only one thing I don't like about it."

"What?"

"It gives you a nice, fat, juicy motive."

When I got back to Piety Street, it was barely midnight and Julian was still awake. He looked me up and down reproachfully.

"Margo, I can see that you are not wearing your girdle."

"It's in my purse." I pulled it out, unrolled it, and flapped it at him. "See? Here it is, safe and sound."

"And why was it in your purse, pray tell?"

"I took it off halfway through the evening."

"I see." He scowled. "Since when do you give up your virginity on the first date?"

"Since I met a very sensible man." I reached behind my neck with both hands, unhooked the necklace, and handed it over.

Julian whistled softly, dragged the prize across his teeth, then held it up to the light to read it, his eyes being younger than mine.

"Mikimoto graded pearls. You must have twisted yourself into a pretzel to earn this little trinket."

"I did. As a bonus, I got some more on the big story."

"Thrill me."

"Martin had known about Delphine cheating Harriet Rosen out of her fortune. She was his aunt, and it was to be his inheritance."

"That would irritate a man. Are you going to tell Frank?"

"Certainly not. Martin told me in bed. Doesn't that make it a privileged communication?"

"Not legally, no. If it was your Romeo who killed Delphine, that pearl necklace is a cheap price to pay for your body *and* your silence."

"He couldn't have done it, anyway. He's too greedy."

"Greediness as an alibi? How plausible."

"In his case, it is. So long as Delphine was alive, she could be convicted of fraud and he could follow the conviction with a civil suit to recover his aunt's capital. But now that Delphine is dead, no conviction is possible and a civil suit against her estate would hardly be feasible. Remember the Rosen money went into the so-called nonprofit corporation."

17

*C*arry on," Julian said. "I was just the driver." He settled on one of Frank's office chairs with such style and grace that he actually looked comfortable and began reading his *Archaeology* magazine.

"All right, Margo," Frank said. "We went over the threatening note, the one Sidney deliberately ignored. The envelope is the kind that come thirty-six to a box in dime stores and supermarkets."

"What can they tell from the note itself."

"Not bloody much. It's from a printer! We used to be able to identify the typewriter that typed a particular letter, easy; there would be a chipped *E* or a high *J* unique to that typewriter. But what do you do with a dot matrix *printer*? There's nothing distinctive about the output!"

"Which font did he use?"

"Courier TrueType. Only the most popular. After our friend printed out the letter, he could simply have overwritten the file, and there would be nothing in the world left for evidence."

"What did you learn from the paper?"

"Oh, that's even cuter. He wouldn't even send us a sample of his own stationary. What we got was actually a photocopy of his letter. And the copy paper is the most common in the country. Here's something else you'll like. While we were sifting through Sidney's receipts, we learned he bought all Delphine's stage makeup at Duchess Theatrical Supplies."

"Nothing strange about that. There are only five of those supply houses in town, and Duchess was closest to his apartment."

Frank shook his head. "The strange part is that Sidney was murdered and someone he knew, the store owner, Mr. Goldstein, became the victim of a murder attempt four days later."

"But Mr. Goldstein said he had an enemy. Some business rival on St. Charles."

"Yes, we interviewed the suspect." The right corner of Frank's mustache turned up. "It transpires that Julius Terwilliger is seventy-five years old and frail as a funeral lily. Even if he could have managed to cock that rifle, the recoil alone would have killed him."

I opened my purse. "Would you give me your take on this? I have a list of people who knew and loved Delphine. Or didn't."

I unfolded the paper on his desk blotter and put my finger on the first name.

"Jake Nesbitt," he said to humor me. "Delphine's P.I."

"He worked undercover, right? And Pluto is the god of the underworld, so there was a connection. But we can forget Nesbitt," I opined. "He had the expertise, but no motive."

"None that we're aware of," Frank amended. "For all you know, he might have been in love with Frieda Harris and gotten angry when she rebuffed him."

"Did you ever see that woman up close in a good light?"

"Only dead."

"She looked no better alive. I can't believe his interest in her was anything but financial. No, he just lost himself a good, steady client."

Frank shrugged, to save an argument without conceding.

"You put down Dan Aparisi."

"Just because he worked in the sewer. Underworld again. But I don't suspect him."

"I don't either. Your next name is Howie Potts, the 'physically challenged' astrologer. He *did* have a motive. He was stuck working for pennies, due to that noncompetition clause in his contract."

"But," I said, "he would have found it *too* 'challenging' to get into his hand-controlled car, drive up to Lakeview, pull out his wheelchair, roll up to Delphine's house, then trick her into a position where he could skewer her with her own sword."

"Not impossible, though. Suppose she was expecting him. Maybe he phoned to say he had a great idea for expansion. Any excuse at all. She said, 'Come on over.' Once in the house, he determined that no one knew he was coming or had seen him arrive. Then he felt safe enough to carry out his plan."

I pointed to the next name. "Andrew Berry had no motive and probably didn't have the physical strength to run through another human being with a sword."

"I'd say it took more skill than strength. If you put the point in the right place, it's all soft tissue."

Frank put a finger of his own on the next name. "Now we come to your friend Martin Koenig. He was in the Marine Corps, so he had the strength and the savvy; no alibi because he lives alone; and he calls his newsletter 'The Pluto Factor.' But . . . " He shrugged. "No decent motive."

I gave out with a noncommittal, "Mmm."

Julian glanced up from his magazine and looked at me hard, but made no comment.

Frank nodded assent to my "Mmm." "Then we have to consider the secretaries, Nona and Didi."

"Neither the strength nor the motive nor the sense."

"I'll agree with that, conditionally. The schoolteacher you interviewed, Mariette Nuñez, has the strength, skill, sense, and motive."

"There's nothing that girl doesn't have. But she didn't do it."

"I think Margo is trying to write her own history here." Julian leaned forward earnestly and put his hand on my knee. "Dear, whom would you *like* it to be?"

"I'd vote for Dr. Ingram."

"I would too," Frank averred, "but that weasel is scared to death of his own wife. You think he would risk facing the law on a murder charge?"

"You know how a doctor gets to thinking he's God."

"A *proctologist* thinks he's God?"

"So they believe they're above the normal human sanctions. He lives within easy walking distance of Delphine. That would account for no one remembering a strange car in the driveway. And he's a proctologist."

"So what that he's a proctologist."

"Pluto rules the excretory system."

"I still think the good doctor is too cowardly to commit murder."

"Okay. My second choice would be Randall Jooby. He knows how to use a sword."

"No motive."

"What if he were blackmailing Delphine?"

"Then he had a motive to keep her alive."

$\mathcal{K}$now what that call was?" I crowed to the company the next afternoon. Julian, Gaby, and Brad looked up from their cards politely.

"What?"

"It looks like our killer of psychics is getting bold. He's warning the press now."

"Press meaning you?" Julian fanned his cards and discarded two.

"Not exactly me personally." I held out the curly fax copy. "Ronnie, the crime editor at the paper, got this note. At first, he thought it was referring to a fraud case."

I put it in the center of the table, and Gaby craned her neck and read it aloud: " 'Da next phony psychic vill be Queen Marie.' Who iss dat?"

"A voodoo practitioner. She's been selling her act locally for nearly a year."

"Queen of what?" Brad asked.

"That's never been discussed. But her gimmick is an interesting one. She pretends to be channeling Marie Laveau"—I took the fourth chair—"whom she claims is her great-great-great-grandmother."

"Try to prove she isn't," Julian said. "The original Marie Laveau had fifteen children. Any black in the hemisphere could be descended from her."

Brad put down his hand. "I'm new in these parts. I've heard about some local legend by that name, but I never read her story."

"I grew up on it," Julian said. "Marie Laveau was a free woman of color who reigned as the Voodoo Queen of New Orleans back in the early eighteen hundreds. Everyone in the region went to consult her. Even the rich white people paid for her potions and powders."

"How'd she promote that?"

"Laveau started out as a hairdresser, and the fine ladies she serviced fed her gossip about all the best families in town. So when she hung out her shingle as a voodooienne, she already had the dope on her prospective clients, and they were convinced that she could read their minds."

"Pretty slick."

Julian nodded. "She used all the magician's tricks they use today, but in a low-tech mode. For example, she didn't have tape recorders to spy on people, but she didn't need them."

"Why not?"

"Remember that in nineteenth-century New Orleans, every middle-class household had black servants, either slave or free."

"I guess they would."

"Marie Laveau would sneak out at night and leave a voodoo doll on some housemaid's front stoop. So the next day, the poor terrified woman would come by weeping that some enemy had put the gris-gris on her, and she would beg Laveau to take the spell off. She didn't have any money to pay for a counterspell, so the price of salvation would be to inform on her masters."

"Vat evil," Gaby said with some feeling.

I said, "No wonder the people were scared of her. She had them believing she couldn't die. When the original Marie Laveau retired in 1869, one of her daughters assumed her name and carried on the franchise." I went to the bookcase for my primary source and held it up. "I read the *Life and Times of Marie Laveau,* which is actually just a handy guide to voodoo spells."

"Vat nonsense!" Gaby sputtered.

I nodded agreement while paging through the book. "Look! Here's a way to make a stingy man spend his money. I have to fill the bathtub halfway with water, then pour in a box of borax, a box of cinnamon, and a cup of sugar. After I take a bath in that solution, the man is supposed to spend everything he has on me."

"Good luck with that, Margo," Julian offered. "As for advertising, Laveau gave the best show in town once a week behind her cottage on St. Ann Street. There would be her dance with her pet snake, Zombi; plenty of tafia, whiskey, and rum; drums beating, shaking the calabash, dancing the bamboula . . . Naturally, they'd decapitate a couple of roosters. And for the finale, she'd present that nadir of debauchery, an orgy under the bushes." He smiled. "It went over very well with the rich and bored. Understand that this was before cable TV."

"So it was all show," Brad said. "She had no real power."

I tapped the book. "Actually, she did have the power to kill your enemy for you. But that power depended upon access to your enemy's food and the fact that forensic science wasn't developed enough to detect most poisons."

"She also had a good sideline arranging romantic encounters between rich white men and poor dark women," Julian added. "All the yellow people you see in this town didn't come from China."

19

*T*he man who opened the door was tall, sealskin black, and beautiful, having the look of a Masai warrior even while shirted in electric blue polyester and trousered in bicycle pants.

"Miz Fortier? Come on in. Ah'm Cecil." Then he looked embarrassed and corrected himself, "*King* Cecil."

"Thrilled to make your acquaintance, Your Majesty."

"Uh, yeah. Well, she's . . . Queen Marie's expectin' you. She be raht out. You kin have a seat anywhey."

I looked around at "anywhey." Queen Marie's temple of worship was a rented house featuring cheap characterless furniture that had been overlaid with the trappings of her persona. The armless, no-color couch had been camouflaged with a black throw printed with crimson dragons. There was a card table in the middle of the room, unsuccessfully disguised with a purple tablecloth. The plywood bookcase was stocked with jars hand-labeled as the voodooiene's essentials: cat bones, war powders, victory oils, chapel bell grease for healing . . . Green candles burned in all four corners of the room. Green for money.

There were three paint-chipped folding chairs pulled up to the card table, and I chose the least rickety.

King Cecil continued to stand uncomfortably, flexing on his feet. He had nothing to say to me but had certainly been ordered to watch that I didn't steal any wax dolls or anger powder.

I, however, being gifted with great social skills, can always make conversation.

"Say, Your Majesty?"

"Yeah?"

"Um . . . What are my chances of being elevated to a peerage?"

"Whut?"

I wondered if he had any function at all aside from the obvious one. The voodoo world is perhaps the only society in which the queen always outranks the king.

"Good afternoon, Mrs. Fortier."

My hostess had appeared between the beaded curtains in the doorway. She was of mixed blood, like her spurious ancestor, and was arrayed as a fabric store's idea of a Haitian priestess, in layers of bright cotton prints.

"Thank you for seeing me," I said graciously. I didn't know what I should call this quack, so hoped she wouldn't notice that I wasn't calling her anything.

"My pleasure." She dismissed her consort, "Cecil, go practice your drums," and took the chair across from mine as His Majesty sprinted away in inarticulate relief. "Now, Mrs. Fortier, your editor, Mr. Dune, mentioned a feature article."

She was well spoken, which is my politically-correct way of saying she sounded white.

"Yes," I enthused. "Felix would like a historical piece for the magazine section. You see, Marie Laveau is as important in our local lore as the duc d'Orleans or Jean Lafitte."

"Yes, we were always very proud of my great-grandmother."

(Uh huh.)

"There's the very hook for the article. That you are upholding Marie Laveau's traditions and practicing the same rituals that made her the most powerful woman in New Orleans one hundred and fifty years ago."

The voodooienne smirked with one side of her mouth.

"Person. The most powerful *person* in New Orleans."

I heard a slow *boom-boom-boom* pulsing from somewhere in the rear of the house, so King Cecil must have been doing his homework.

"My great-grandmother was an eminent humanitarian. I hope to carry on the same good works."

"Yes, indeed!" (I was willing to shovel some her way.) "She offered help and advice to the poor and desperate, and I've heard that you do the same. What kind of people call on you?"

"Most of my clients are unemployed people needing funds. And then there are the young girls in love."

I seized on that. "What about middle-aged women in love?"

Queen Marie narrowed her eyes, now suspecting that my mission could be other than professional. "I can help them too."

"Just speaking hypothetically and using . . . well . . . myself as an example, what would you advise if there were a certain gentleman I wanted to attract?"

"I have just the prescription, hypothetically, of course." She rose with grace she didn't have to choreograph and selected a vial of a pink substance labeled LOVE POWDER. I took it from her hand, pulled the cork out, and sniffed. I'd guess it to be dime-store talcum dyed with food coloring and scented with cheap perfume.

"If you rub that on your man while he sleeps," she assured, "he will feel very great passion for you."

(Were I in a position to rub anything on a man while he slept, I should think the "passion" part would have been a foregone conclusion.)

I handed the vial back. "There's no problem with that area of the relationship."

"I see." She tapped her smooth brow, as though reading my mind. "If you want to keep this man forever . . . " She put three lavender candles in front of me. "Light these and pray to Onzoncaire. Then you have to mix your blood with black ink and write the man's name nine times on a piece of paper. He will never be able to leave you."

"Never?" (Cripes!) "What about after I get tired of him?"

"Then if you don't want that man anymore, I can give you some 'Go Away' powder that you can throw in his face."

The rule is that potions and powders that are supposed to do good must smell nice. Products prepared for an evil purpose are made to smell vile. The traditional formula for "Go Away" powder was a compound of road dirt, gunpowder, and pepper. And if you throw something like that in anybody's face, his immediate instinct will be (by George!) to "Go Away."

I wondered if it would work with Hubie Nadler.

"Queen Marie," I said earnestly, resorting to her self-bestowed royal address. "There's a man who has tried to kill me."

The voodooienne held her hands out and wiggled her fingers. "Yes. I feel some evil spirit around you."

"Do you have any protection against great bodily harm among your arsenal?"

She pretended to think it over. "I'm not sure my gris-gris will be strong enough, so you are to pay me only if it works."

"That sounds very fair," I deadpanned.

"I'll give you a conjure ball." She went back to her stock and fetched a golf ball–sized sphere rolled from black candle wax and stuck with pins. "This has been marked with human blood and empowered with a spell. You must roll it across the yard of your enemy during the night. That will bring about his death or some other great misfortune within the household."

"Nifty," I said.

"Look here, Julian. This is the big gris-gris."

I stooped in front of the kitchen fireplace, placed the newspaper-wrapped package on the hearth, and managed, without touching the conjure ball, to pull the paper aside and display it for him.

"That little blob of wax is supposed to work magic?"

"It's all in the promise. If, during the normal course of events, anybody in 'my enemy's' house gets sick or has an accident, I'll be convinced Queen Marie's gris-gris worked and bring her my money. If it doesn't happen, she's only out a little candle wax and some pins."

"You're not likely to complain to the consumer advocates, either," Julian allowed. He raised his voice to a whiny falsetto. " 'I pushed that hoodoo ball back and forth in front of my neighbor's house all night long, and nobody inside even got a *cold*.' "

"So she can't lose." I picked up the fireplace tongs. "She said a prayer calling on a 'Papa En Bas.' You ever hear of a saint by that name?"

"*En Bas* means 'below,' my dear. That 'saint' she called on would be the Devil himself."

"That's what I was afraid of."

"The problem is that sometimes those fetishes appear to bring about the desired consequences."

"It's all within the realm of possibility. Nobody knows the power of the mind." I refolded the piece of newspaper around the ball, stood up, and stomped the whole thing flat.

"But suppose it does work? Any way you cause evil, the evil comes back on you. With interest."

I used the fireplace tongs to pick up the conjure ball and toss it into the gray cinders. Then I ignited it with a kitchen match and fed in more newspaper till it burned brightly and the wax melted and dribbled through the ashes in a transparent stream.

"Margo, you are the most superstitious skeptic I've ever seen."

20

*M*artin let me pick my mocha layer cake out of the box and selected a cream puff for himself.

In reaching for the forks, he leaned toward me and inhaled.

"You smell like . . . cinnamon?"

"And sugar and borax. I took a bath in the stuff."

"That sounds like a pretty strange treatment."

"I know, but it's supposed to help me get some new hats at Fleur de Paris."

"Why bother with all that crap? I'll buy you the hats."

(Aha! It worked!)

"I've been worried about you risking your soft white ass over this murder story. You can't spend every waking hour with me, Julian, or some cop."

"I've got something almost as good." I reached into my purse and pulled out the catalog. "Look here. There's this dummy I can send for. See it comes in white or black and looks very realistic."

"A dummy?! So what? Are you going into ventriloquism?"

"No, silly. The idea is that I can dress it any way I like, prop it up in the passenger seat of my car, and people will think I have a male companion."

"But what kind of male companion? Some wimp who lets his woman do the driving!" He pounded the counter. "Listen, Margo. Dump the story. It's not worth your life."

"Never mind. That killer isn't thinking about me. The latest phony psychic to be threatened is someone who calls herself Queen Marie."

"That hoodoo broad? Now there's a target I'll endorse. She's been running a scam on my poor old cleaning woman, Mrs. Givers."

My fork stopped in midair. "What kind of scam?"

"A real nasty one. Mrs. Givers has custody of her three-year-old granddaughter, Saleesha. She's stuck with her. The kid's mother died in a car accident, and, of course, there never was a father."

"Parthenogenesis being rampart among the urban poor."

"Right. To add to the problem, little Saleesha is always coming down with something. Every bug and virus that hits the city is bound to get this kid first: coughs, earaches, runny nose, whatever you can think of. So I got her birth data and checked the natal chart. Surprise! She has a loaded sixth house."

"So there were bound to be health problems."

"Sure, but just minor ailments, nothing life threatening. I tried to tell Mrs. Givers that, but do you think she'd listen? Hell, no. She'd rather believe in curses."

"I'd like to talk to that lady."

"No problem." Martin looked at his watch. "She should be here with her mop and pail inside fifteen minutes."

Mrs. Givers was a small, wiry laboring woman with a complexion like beef jerky and a curly brown acrylic wig. Her lifetime of selfless toil and responsibility had shriveled her like the Sibyl.

She was willing to repeat her story for me, perched on the edge of a kitchen chair with her pail at her feet.

"Mah neighbah Doris done tole me Queen Marie was the on'y one who could mebbe he'p me. So ah made an apperntment. Took de Franklin Street bus over ta her house."

"She managed to convince you that she was sincere."

"Oh yeah, Queen Marie show'd she got de powah o' healin', fust thing. When ah went ta see her, ah had me dis bad headache. So she say she was gwine fix me up a potion. An' she done carried it in from de kitchen all fizzin' an' poppin'. Tole me ta drink it raht down, an' ah did. Taste kinda lahk cherry." Mrs. Givers slapped her bony knee. "Well, don't you know in jes' a few minutes mah ole head was feelin' purty good!"

"I'm sure."

(I could produce exactly the same effect. My "potion" would be a glass of cherry cola with an Alka-Seltzer and a couple of aspirins dissolved therein.)

"Ah tole her as how my grandbaby, Saleesha, kep' gittin' sick. Ah mean ever' week it was somethin', a earache dat kep' de poor chile up all naht or a vahrus or constipation, see? So ah carried her up ta de doctah, but all he done was make some o' his fancy tests an' den come back an' say nothin' was really wrong wit' Saleesha. So dis las' tahm mah li'l baby got sick, ah was raht desperat' an' come ta Queen Marie ta get a powdah or somethin'. She turn de laht out an' went inna trancet raht dey in her livin' room an' called on de spirit o' Marie Laveau. Ah heard de voice mahse'f."

"Sort of like an echo?"

"Yeah. Dats jes' how she sound."

(A reverberator being a cheap and easy effect.)

Mrs. Givers spread her hands, as though accepting a mystical visitation. "Marie Laveau, she say it seems lahk dey was a heap o' money associated wit' someone who's dead. Dat was attractin' evil spirits ta de chile."

"And did you have a large amount of money?"

"You know what? De Queen done ast me dat very question. So ah esplain'd as how mah daughtah Loretta had died inna accident two years ago an' dey was some insurance made out ta me, fifteen thousan' dollahs. Ah put ten down on mah li'l house on Pauger Street an' de res' went in de bank an' ah ain't touched it sence."

At this point, I could have filled in the rest of the story myself, but I let her go on with it.

"Den Queen Marie tole me how she had ta tes' mah money ta see if dats what was makin' de bad gris-gris."

"And how was she going to test it?"

Mrs. Givers searched her recollections. "All ah needed ta do was take a fresh egg out mah refrigahratah an' put it undah mah pilla wit' de bankbook. Den de nex' week, ah brung her dat egg an' she broke it inna dish . . . " The poor woman knotted her arms together and shuddered.

"There was a human skull inside the egg?" I suggested. "The skull of a shrunken head?"

Mrs. Givers gasped. "You know! Dats jes' what it was!"

"So now you were convinced the insurance money was cursed."

"Curs'd, yeah, it hadda be! 'Cause it came outta mah poor daughtah's dyin'!" She bent over nearly double and folded her arms across her thin chest. "Queen Marie said de house was pourin' its evil all ovah mah Saleesha an' mebbe ah'd hafta burn de whole thing down ta save her!"

Tears welled in her eyes, and she pulled a wad of tissue from the pocket of her moth-eaten cardigan. A loop of plastic glow-in-the-dark rosary beads came out with it. She poked the beads back in and blew her nose.

Martin had managed to keep silent during this story, but at this point, he looked ready to shoot missiles with his eyes.

I prompted the witness. "But then she found another solution, didn't she?"

"Yeah." Mrs. Givers kept her voice even. Self-pity being an indulgence her kind can't afford. "Den Queen Marie say mebbe she can take de curse off so at leas' ah can keep mah home. Ah jes' hafta bring her de money dats lef' in de bank. Den she's gwine make a blessin' on mah house, an' it'll be all raht an' we can still live dey. Ah was savin' dat money ta send Saleesha up ta college. But what good is college if mah precious chile is daid!"

"I can help." I put a hand on her thin shoulder. "You don't have to go back to Queen Marie."

"No, ah gots ta bring her de money. She warn me."

"Please, just give me a couple of days to prove it to you. If my way doesn't work, you can try her way."

The woman looked over to Martin, who nodded vigorously then shrugged. "Mebbe two days."

"Good! Now what is your saint name?"

"Saint name? Oh, dey baptahz'd me as Theresa."

Theresa? Great! I actually clapped my hands. "That's very fortunate, Mrs. Givers. Listen, you don't have to take any money out of the bank. Just go straight to Saint Theresa of Lisieux, the Little Flower of Jesus. She has much more power than any living person."

The woman didn't answer but just nodded. The greater power of the dead couldn't be disputed.

"Saint Theresa always helps people who ask. So you must visit her at her own church, which is on the thirty-eight hundred block of Leonidas."

"Ah kin take de bus."

"I'll drive her," Martin said peremptorily.

"Fine." I gave him a discreet thumbs-up signal, then turned back to the old woman. "You must light a candle in front of her statue and say your rosary." I held up a finger. "All fifteen decades."

"Yeah?" Mrs. Givers hadn't stopped nodding.

"The Little Flower can intercede for you so your grandchild's life won't be in danger."

"But what if she won't he'p us? How kin ah tell?"

The woman's permanently worried brow had wrinkled even further.

"If she decides to answer your prayer, Saint Theresa will let you know by sending a rose."

"Send me a rose? She do dat?"

"Yes, you will get a rose in some form during the next two days."

Mrs. Givers nodded once more, decisively. "Ah will go ta dat church an' say dat rosary ta Saint Theresa. Den ah'll go raht on home an' wait on mah rose. Oh, thanks be ta God!"

Martin and I adjourned to his office and left Mrs. Givers to her work. I closed the door behind us and took the leather couch.

"I swear, I don't know why people keep falling for those gypsy cons. Their tricks have been exposed in the media hundreds of times."

Martin settled in his swivel chair. "So, okay, I figure she palmed the disgusting thing, then dropped it into the dish while she was breaking the egg. But . . . where could Queen Marie have gotten hold of a shrunken human skull?"

"That would be kind of hard to come up with. So she probably just took the skull of a chicken and broke off the beak."

"That would look human?"

"Enough to convince Mrs. Givers. She would hardly pick it up and carry it off to a lab."

Martin reached over and patted my knee. "Good strategy, dear. You fight Queen Marie's superstition with an older, more powerful superstition."

"I fight black magic with white magic. Thank the Lord she's Catholic. Protestants don't have any saints to call on."

"Jews don't either."

"You kidding? You've got Jesus Christ himself!"

"I don't think he's been too thrilled with us ever since that crucifixion thing."

21

I've been reading up, Frank. Queen Marie claims she was born in a little village on one of the islands."

"And so she was." He dug under a pile on his desk and came up with a computer readout. "On the island of Manhattan. The little village is known as Harlem."

"You're way ahead of me."

"Way. She was born Alison Williams in 1949. Her mother was a schoolteacher who died young, and her father a pharmacist."

"Then she wasn't brought up in some primitive milieu of ignorance and superstition."

"Hardly. Two years at Hunter College, then a short stint as an Alvin Ailey dancer. She lost that gig when she developed a nose problem."

"Cocaine?"

"That's how she first got involved with the law. According to her sheet, NYPD picked her up for possession once. There was no honest way to make enough money to support her nose, so she invented this voodoo scam. Williams was run out of Harlem in '89."

"By the police?"

"No, we don't have the power to do that. The word was that she stung some gang kid's mother for her life savings. All mothers look alike, right? How was she to know?"

"You contacted her about the threatening letter?"

"Immediately."

"What was her attitude?"

"Dismissive. I offered her police protection, but she turned it down."

"Just like that?"

"Miss Williams says she's threatened by evil forces all the time, but her power will always safeguard her."

"I don't get why she would take a chance with her life?"

"Think, Margo. Her whole enterprise depends on sustaining the illusion of power. If she can't protect *herself* from harm, how can she do it for the paying customers? And there's also the fact that many of Miss Williams's followers spend most of their waking time avoiding the police."

I said, "I've got a great idea for a cheap way of furnishing protection."

"What would that be?"

"Why don't you just arrest her ass and put it away in a nice safe jail."

"Arrest it for what?"

"I was thinking about fraud."

"What's fraudulent about performing under a stage name? Because she does some silly dance with a snake, Miss Williams gets to classify herself as an entertainer. She may charge admission for her 'performances.' "

"But she's trying to con an old woman out of her life savings. There must be something in the law about that."

"Right. So bring that woman in here, Margo. Bring *anyone* in here to make a statement, and I'll have Miss Williams booked."

"You know her victims are too scared. She threatened to curse their grandchildren with a wasting disease."

"Naturally. Her business is to prey on the ignorant."

"If you caught her taking people's money, wouldn't you arrest her?"

"I don't think she'll do it in front of me."

"Maybe she will. Mrs. Givers told me Queen Marie is having a wealth ceremony tomorrow night."

" 'Wealth ceremony'? It sounds like one of those yuppie motivational seminars. Where is she holding it?"

"The cemetery, natch. You're going to have to go undercover. Try to look like a poor working-class man."

"I *am* a poor working-class man. Why in the cemetery?"

"Where else? The first two Marie Laveaus performed their disgusting rituals in their cottage at ten-twenty St. Ann Street, but that building was razed to the ground in 1903."

Frank put his hand on the mail in his in-box and picked up the envelope on top. "What a shame." He pulled the flap open and drew out the letter. "This is from a *dating* service," he growled. "Who the hell thinks I can afford a *date*?!" He put the letter together with the envelope, tore them in half, and dropped them in the circular file to join other unwanted and similarly dealt-with communications.

"Funny," I said. "Sidney got the same ad and reacted the same— No, he didn't!"

"Hmm?" Frank was on to the next letter in the stack.

"You rip your mail in half before throwing it away."

"Right." He demonstrated again by tearing up a generous offer from Ed McMahon.

"But Sidney didn't do that. I saw him throw his junk mail away whole."

"So?"

"So this could be the answer to our big mystery. Why didn't Sidney tell the police he'd gotten a threatening note? Because he never got one."

Frank raised his eyebrows. "Hey, that's *good*. Someone mailed Sidney that envelope in advance, with nothing of consequence in it. Maybe an ad."

"Just to get the right postmark. And . . . and . . . " I bounced in my seat. "After he killed Sidney, he fished the envelope—whole—out of Sidney's wastebasket and slipped in the threatening note."

"But why?"

"He wanted the glory of sending a warning without the risk of an actual warning."

22

St. Louis Cemetery No. 1 is a magnet for tourists. But we locals give the place wide berth. The evil creatures we fear are not ghosts but fleshly demons who would happily make ghosts of any of us for the price of a vial of crack.

I walked around the bank of broken glass, the remains of the car windows of oblivious tourists.

The cemetery's main drawing card is a limestone family mausoleum constructed more than a hundred years ago:

FAMILLE VVE PARIS

NÉE LAVEAU

CI—GÎT

MARIE PHILOME GLAPION

DÉCÉDÉE LE 11 JUIN 1897

AGÉE DE SOIXANTE-deux ANS ELLE FUT

BONNE MÈRE, BONNE AMIE, ET

REGRETTÉE PAR TOUS CEUX QUI L'ONT

CONNUE PASSANTE PRIEZ POUR ELLE.

The dates refer to the second Marie. Her mother had been forgotten by the time the tomb was inscribed, but she's in there too.

The tomb of Marie Laveau, as always, had little crosses all over it, penciled in by supplicants who were asking favors of her spirit. They would knock on the slab three times, then burn a candle and leave their gifts in the flower holders that are attached to each side of the tomb.

I was occupied in deciphering the French when I felt a hand on my shoulder.

"S'cuz me, miz?"

I glanced behind me and saw a large black man carrying a brown paper bag. I flinched away from his touch, at the same time clamping my hand down on my hip pocket and yelling, "Hey!"

He grinned. "You didn't recognize me."

Then I saw that it was only good old Frank, wearing jeans, a cheap windbreaker, and worn jogging shoes.

"Well...uh...Sure, I recognized you." I took my hand off my pocket. "I've always been afraid you'd lift my wallet. Where did you get the snappy threads?"

"These are my off-duty clothes. What did you think I wear around the house?"

"I always figured that when you take your suit and tie off at night, there's another suit and tie underneath." Then I whispered, "Where's your gun?"

"In this paper bag, along with my radio. Duffy's tuned in outside the gates." Frank pointed at the tomb and shook his head. "Look at all those stubs of red candle. Like votive offerings. Who could believe that *she* made it to sainthood?"

"Not God's side. The other camp."

I looked around at the throng of believers—some old, perhaps looking for a supernatural rejuvenation; some crippled, walking with canes and crutches while they prayed for a miracle of wholebodiedness; and those whose problems couldn't immediately be discerned, the financially or emotionally bankrupt. "I'm surprised at all the white people I see here."

Frank grunted. "You think only blacks are ignorant?"

At that moment, we heard a stirring in the crowd behind us that made us whirl around. Queen Marie had just entered the cemetery, her cotton prints fluttering in the cold night breeze as she carried an elaborately carved box that she had probably bought at Pier 1. Her "king," Cecil, walked behind her holding out a woven basket, which at a closer look seemed to be moving, breathing.

Other faithful acolytes, male and female, followed in line, bearing congo drums, bottles, bowls, and calabashes.

The pretender to the throne of Marie Laveau took a central position in front of the tomb, while Cecil folded his limbs on the ground behind her and began beating the congo drum. The acolytes shrugged off their clothing and began stamping and undulating with the steady rhythms.

Frank frowned. "Those male dancers are getting too close."

"Well," I assured him, "they sure couldn't be hiding any knives, could they? They're naked."

"Obviously."

"So if they poked her with *anything,* it would have to be—"

"Yes, yes . . ."

In a grand theatrical gesture, the voodooienne pulled open the lid of the carved box and lifted out a big fat boa constrictor. The people closest to her drew back in horror as she wrapped it around her body, holding the snake's face up to hers so it could lick her cheek with its forked tongue. A loud gasp issued from the assemblage.

(Big deal. Boas aren't poisonous.)

Next she yanked off the top of the basket and pulled out a black chicken with its feet tied together. It cackled and tried to flap its wings, but she held it tightly and picked up the wooden bowl.

"King" Cecil had stopped thumping by now and pulled a long knife out from behind his drum. Frank started forward, but I held him back and whispered, "The knife is for the rooster, not her."

"What? Oh, yes. Of course."

Cecil took the chicken from her and held it over the bowl while Queen Marie wielded the knife. Hers was the honor of cutting the bird's throat so its blood flowed into the bowl.

The voodooienne then offered the bowl around, and those closest to her drank from it as the chicken's now-headless body hopped and twisted. I backed up well out of the way of the splattering. I like my dead chickens cooked.

Frank covered his eyes to hide a grimace and hissed.

"This is horrible!"

"Tame stuff," I hissed back. "The original Laveau used to boil a live black cat."

"No!"

The sacrifices always had to be black: a black goat, a black cat, a black chicken. Not a lucky color for God's creatures.

Cecil resumed his position behind his drum, and the voodooienne began to dance, throwing her arms out, writhing sinuously.

The drummer began chanting:

> *"Eh! Eh! Bomba hen hen!*
> *Canga bafie te*
> *Danga moune de te*
> *Canga do ki li!*
> *Canga li!"*

Then, all in one motion, the dancer unwound the multifabric dress and held a stunning pose, wearing only a loincloth of knotted red silk handkerchiefs.

Frank murmured, "She sure is beautiful."

I myself wasn't distracted. "If evil can be beautiful."

"It can."

"My faithful people, we will bring you riches!" she proclaimed. "But first we must plant the seeds of wealth!"

There was whooping and shouting around us as the future million-aires crowded forward to hear planting instructions. Two of the naked assistants spread a red polyester blanket on the ground in front of their priestess.

"And now my people," she shouted, "you must put your money into the blanket. If you want the spirits to bring you one hundred dollars, you must plant ten. If you want a thousand, you must plant one hundred."

The faithful began digging in their pockets and purses.

137

Queen Marie threw her long arms straight out in a cruciform.

"And now, my people, I call down—"

In that instant, I saw a red blotch appear on her chest and then bubble and spread. I assumed it was part of the act and was admiring the effect till Queen Marie jerked back then fell forward with a complete lack of grace. Some of the people closest to her screamed.

Frank bolted out of character, ran to the middle of the circle, and knelt beside her. In a flash, he pulled out his leather badge case and flipped it open. "Nobody move!"

He might as well have been speaking Swahili. Every man and woman in sight, including the faithful "King" Cecil, picked up their traps and took off running in the spirit of "Feets don't fail me now!" There never was a crowd of poor, old, and infirm people who moved so fast.

I was quick enough to jump behind a tomb as the herd stampeded past, and so saved myself from being trampled flat. Within less than a minute, Frank and I were the only living souls left in the cemetery alongside one freshly dead one.

Frank pulled his radio out of the paper bag and clicked it on. "Duffy? You out there . . . ? You're going to hate this."

"It had to be a rifle shot, fired from over that Iberville Street wall, but the M.E. will tell us for sure."

"Makes sense, Frank." Duffy turned on his radio and moved over to the gate to speak into it.

By now, there were three units on the scene and plastic evidence bags were being flapped around.

Frank set his jaw. "I came down here to prevent her from being killed by a sword or a knife, then all of a sudden she gets hit by a bullet! Why did the killer change his M.O.?"

"Because he couldn't get close enough to use a blade," I reasoned.

"Serial killers usually stick to one method. I don't like this."

"Maybe this murder is just a bizarre coincidence," I said brightly.

"Too bizarre for my money."

I pulled my coat tight around me. "Come to think of it, this murder looks more like . . . but that couldn't possibly be connected."

"What couldn't be connected?"

"Remember the other day, when I was riding with Officer Gendron? Someone shot at the proprietor of a theatrical makeup shop but missed. He also used a rifle."

"But did that intended victim have any connection to Queen Marie that you can fathom?"

"Goldstein? No." I shook my head. "There may be some Jew somewhere who's into voodoo, but I never heard of one."

"Me neither. New Orleans voodoo is a grotesque and mutated offshoot of the Christian religion."

"Hey, Frank!" Duffy waved his flashlight. "Something I want to show you." The flashlight beam traveled down the side of the tomb, over the inevitable defacement of penciled crosses, to a different kind of mark at the base. "Where did you see that before?"

Frank squatted to examine it. "The same symbol we saw at the other two murder scenes."

"The glyph for Pluto," I said.

"Maybe."

"So when did he put it there?"

"I doubt the rifleman is still skulking around the neighborhood." Frank took Duffy's hand to hoist himself up. "He must have come here earlier today and scratched it in. We didn't see it in the dark."

"No one would have noticed."

*S*o, Julian, another phony psychic has been killed off. I've got to get in on this."

"Really? I should think you would feel uncomfortable killing a phony psychic."

"Not killing one, nudnick, *being* one."

"You perceive a shortage?"

"Don't you see a pattern emerging? There's a serial killer somewhere who has it in for phony psychics, and the best way to catch him is to become a target."

"To become the fourth fatality in the series? What fun! Does your faithful husband have any input as to this project?"

"No."

"I thought not."

"And I've got the perfect opportunity. Delphine's next scheduled appearance was for the Regional Exploration Convention."

"An industrial show?"

"Those presentations get very expensive. They had mounted a full-scale stage production to demonstrate her powers. The Mystic Sidney was going to do the show, but he'll probably have to skip it now."

"No doubt. So?"

"So, *I'll* just slip into the gig."

"Armed with no more than what you learned from peeking behind the curtain at the Follies Club?"

"I'll have more than that. It's all arranged. Andrew knows everything there is to know about the stagecraft." I sashayed over to the mirror and took a theatrical stance. "And he's offered to provide the wardrobe and manage the backstage operation, while I take the starring role out front."

"The little rodent must really be scraping out the barrel for talent."

"Rather, he's really committed to helping me find out who killed his friend."

"And meal ticket. But even with Andrew's help, you're hardly qualified to go on for Mystic Delphine . . . or even for Mystic *Sidney.*"

I lifted a tress of my crown hair and laid it down carefully to simulate fullness. "You seem to forget that I already have two years' experience performing onstage in costume."

"No, my dear, I didn't forget. But considering that said stage was behind the bar at Madame Julie's and said 'performance' consisted mainly of removing said costume, I'd hardly call you an heir to Bernhardt and Duse."

"The best part is, I don't *have* to act; I'll just be my normal winsome self. As for the psychic connection, I already have a reputation around town for reading cards at parties."

"And I for balancing a penny on the end of my nose, but no one would pay to see me do it."

"Julian, this is my chance to make the big time as an investigative reporter. When Opportunity comes knocking, I have to open the door."

"How do you know whether it's Opportunity knocking or just one of those Jehovah's Witnesses?"

I didn't answer, because I was busy punching a number.

"Hello, Gaby! Do you have a good head for figures?"

"Off course, darlink. I'm German. Vy?"

"Because you're going to clinch my finale."

The Regional Exploration Convention was provided by the company as recreation and reward for high-performing employees. I had second billing in the entertainment portion, after a nerdy motivational speaker and before a waddle of gospel singers.

The announcer for the event was the Regional Exploration CEO, the full-of-himself Charleton Pierce.

"And now for our distinguished audience of REC's very highest achievers, we are presenting the astonishing mental permutations of the Mystic Margo!"

With that, I sashayed out onstage in my best shocking pink push-up gown.

The applause was moderate. This was an "Oh, yeah? So *show* me!" kind of reception.

Pierce picked a pool stenographer for the first reading, and she stood up somewhat shyly.

I closed my eyes and went into my act. "Do you know someone . . . His name starts with a *J*. Yes . . . " I flailed at the air. "His name is John or Jim or Joe . . . "

(Only the most common men's names in the English-speaking world.)

"Yes, I do," she gasped. "My ex-boyfriend, Johnny!"

"He still misses you."

"That's funny. He dumped me for that waitress."

"But do not return to him."

"I *wouldn't*."

"I see another man, much more suitable."

"You mean Mitch?"

"Starts with an *M* . . . Yes, Mitch! He truly admires you."

"He should. We're going to get married in June."

The next querent sounded sixty years old, so there would be no Johnnies or Mitches for her.

"I see health concerns. You or someone very close." (Who doesn't have health concerns?)

"That's *right*," came the amazed reply. "I'm going to the doctor tomorrow morning!"

I put my hands up in front of my face and peeked out at the woman, who looked sound as an ox and about as wide.

"Yes . . . he will tell you something about . . . He'll want you to change. He'll give you a printed piece of paper." (Like maybe a *diet* sheet?)

And so the act continued for the next twenty minutes, with the subjects inadvertently leading me into saying what they wanted to hear, until it was time for the clincher.

For this bit, Andrew appeared onstage, pushing a green chalkboard. He pulled himself up to his full height. What there was of it. (According to Miss Georgia, "Leave terms like 'short,' 'shrimpy,' 'runty,' and 'diminutive' out of your vocabulary. Gentlemen are to be described as 'compactly built,' while ladies are 'petite.' ")

"Now, distinguished members of the audience," he declaimed. "This is the grand finale of the demonstration. At this time, Mrs. Fortier will take numbers from the assemblage. To assist in this demonstration, we call upon the First Lady of Regional Exploration. Mrs. Ada Pierce, will you please join us onstage."

The CEO's wifey wife, billowing in a print shirtwaist, made her way up the steps amid mandatory applause. Obviously his first wife, I thought. Rich men either get themselves a series of wives, or more sensibly, they hold on to the same wife, children, and house and keep the hormones popping with a series of mistresses.

"For the first figure,"—I directed my voice upward to the boom mike—"pick any number from one to nine. Mrs. Pierce, you may choose anyone on the left side of the auditorium."

"Very well," she twittered as hands shot up. "You there, Franny?" Franny, a matron of comparable deterioration, heaved out of her seat, proud of the distinction.

"Five!" she hollered. "I choose *five*!"

"Five it is."

Using her best Palmer penmanship, Ada drew the numeral in the upper right corner of the chalkboard.

I continued, "Now from the right side of the room, would you choose someone with a number from ten through ninety-nine."

Ada tasted her power before cocking her head at a lanky man, who contributed fifty-six then officiously drew the number under the five.

I touched my temples, to look mental. "On the left side, someone is thinking of a number between one hundred and nine hundred ninety-nine."

Apparently several were. But the person who called out 163 was probably a friend of Ada's, so she waved and added that number to the board. "It's getting big," she said.

I nodded, in deep concentration. "Please pick someone in the rear who will give you a number between one thousand and nine thousand, nine hundred, and ninety-nine."

There was some hesitation while the crowd in the rear tried to find one soul among them who could conceive of a number that high. But finally, one bold man waved a whiskey glass for attention. "Eight thousand and thirty."

Ada nodded in relief and added his number to the column, no doubt hoping that her part of the performance was over. But I persisted once more.

"And now, somewhere on the aisle, a lady has a number between ten thousand and ninety-nine thousand, nine hundred, and ninety-nine."

"Fourteen thousand, nine hundred, und thirty-one," shrilled a woman in an orange scarf and a purple trench coat.

Ada was more than happy to add that five-digit number to the board. Then she stood away from it and put down her chalk in a final gesture.

Andrew stepped up again.

"Now to show there is no collusion, we will call on the Regional Exploration Company's head bookkeeper. Mr. Alvin Simmons, would you please step up here and do the addition?"

"Yes, certainly. Ahem."

Simmons made his way up onstage. He looked fairly competent. I hoped so. If the numbers weren't added right, I was porked.

Mr. Simmons cocked his head back to read through the lower lenses of his bifocals, then took the chalk, added the numbers precisely, and solemnly announced the sum. "That would be twenty-three thousand, one hundred eighty-five!"

I turned to Mr. Pierce. "And now will you produce the envelope that has been in your care since four o'clock."

The CEO waved at his assistant. "Mrs. Curtis? You have the envelope I gave you this afternoon?"

Mrs. Curtis came forward, grim-lipped with reverence for her commission. I tried to seem mystical without looking downright bored as a table knife was produced to open the envelope, which had been wrapped three times with mailing tape. Then she gasped with astonishment as she held up the paper for all to see.

"Why, it's twenty-three thousand, one hundred eighty-five! Just like on the board!"

After just one second of silent amazement, applause rocked the auditorium.

I got up and bowed, which I do better than anything else, then feigning shyness and mental exhaustion, carried my fat butt off the stage.

Frank was waiting back in the dressing room to hand me my wet towel. "My Lord, Margo. I was almost ready to believe you're psychic."

"You know very well I'm not." I wiped off my hot stage makeup. "Or I would have bought Chrysler at six."

"Then how did you project your thoughts into that envelope at the end of your act?"

"I didn't." He looked painfully curious, so I gave it away. "The twenty-three thousand, one hundred eighty-five was a predetermined figure. I just wrote it down this afternoon and sealed it in the envelope in front of Mr. Pierce."

"But those people in the audience were members of the sponsor's organization. How did you get them all to pick the right numbers?"

"Not all, Frank, just one. The last one. And here she is."

Frank didn't recognize the woman in the ugly purple trench coat until she took off her scarf.

"Gaby?"

She held her hand out. "Goot evening, Lieutenant."

"You see?" I patted her shoulder. "I got Gaby a ticket for the show, then she came in early. No one questioned her presence because everyone just assumed she was someone else's mother. So she sat on the aisle, with the predetermined number in her mind. Then, whenever a number was accepted from the audience and written on the board, my confederate here simply mentally subtracted it from the original one. When I asked for the final number, I just indicated Gaby's section of the room and she was ready before anyone else was."

He whistled low. "To sing out that one number which, added to all the others, would total your predetermined figure."

"Presto."

Outside on the banquette, Frank watched me field congratulations for a show well done. I had waved a cheery bye to the last fan when Andrew joined us, rubbing his hands together.

"That was a great show, Margo!"

I was modest. "It's so easy to fool people who want to be fooled. I mean, they'll meet you ninety percent of the way."

"Right. You proved you can impress an audience. Now we're ready for the second phase."

Frank and I looked at each other. "What second phase?"

"Well, tonight's performance was good, but it just established you as a mentalist like Kreskin. If you want to get a reputation as a psychic, you've got to go beyond mind-reading tricks."

"Beyond to what?"

"How about channeling?"

"Holy cow!"

"See, that was how Delphine made her name." Andrew used his index finger to trace a marquee with a name spelled out in lightbulbs. "You have to present yourself as a medium. We'll say you're allowing your body and voice to be used as a means of communication from a departed spirit."

Frank wrinkled his nose. "You mean play the part of a dead person?"

"But the dead person of her *choice,* Lieutenant. Anyone from Cleopatra to Betsy Ross." Andrew held his palms out. "Piece of cake."

Frank batted the idea aside. "That's impossible. Margo isn't an actress."

"Hey, I can get in character right here. Dig this. I'll bet I can channel my favorite movie star!"

Andrew beamed. "Go to it."

I pushed out my chest, pursed my lips, and breathed my line from *Gentlemen Prefer Blondes,* articulating each consonant.

" 'Yew might not marry a girl just because she's pretty, but my goodness"—here I fluttered my lashes—"doesn't it help?' "

Frank looked pained. "Who is that? Bogart?"

Andrew shook his head. "I had Eddie Cantor. Look, Margo, maybe you would be better advised to channel an entity who isn't so famous."

"One who isn't familiar," Frank offered.

"One nobody ever heard of at all," Andrew suggested. "A make-believe person."

"Make-believe?" I was about to make a rejoinder to that when I was distracted by a small black woman hurrying toward me.

I didn't recognize her until she clutched my hand and said, "Oh, thank you, Miz Fortier! Ah got mah rose!"

"Your rose? Oh, good evening, Mrs. Givers!"

"Yeah, Mr. Martin, he drove me ovah dey to Saint Theresa's church on Leonidas, an' ah done knelt down in front o' dat statue an' say de rosary jes' lahk you tole me an' she sho'nuff answered. De very nex' mohnin' mah sistah had sent me a lettah, an' de papah had dis li'l pink rose raht dey in de middle."

"Well." I smiled. "That's as clear as it can be."

She took my hand in both of hers. "Saint Theresa an' me're gwine take care o' mah baby grandchile *togethah*. So ah know if she gits a sniffle it's jes' gwine be a sniffle lahk othah kids git. 'Cause she's safe from now on."

She squeezed my hand and turned quickly. The St. Claude Avenue bus had just pulled up to the curb, and she had to hurry to join the line of passengers.

Frank leaned toward me and whispered, "How did you manage that?"

"What?"

"Getting Mrs. Givers's sister to send her a note with a rose on it?"

"Oh, I didn't have to. Saint Theresa always sends a rose."

Julian shook his head over his martini.

"So you are supposed to play the part of an imaginary dead person? That's ridiculous. You could never be anyone but yourself."

"But listen, I could play a turn-of-the-century Irish woman. Remember, I do a pretty good brogue."

"In the Irish Channel on Saint Paddy's Day. That hardly makes you Maureen O'Hara."

"I don't have to make like a movie star. See, I've got it all figured. I only need to write out a plausible scenario for the channeled entity."

"And how do you manage that so quickly?"

I walked to the mantle and picked up the grainy portrait of Granny Armaugh and the four-year-old me.

"I'm halfway there. I can be her."

"Your great-grandmother?"

"Her maiden name was Mavourneen Rose Kerrigan. She used to tell me all about her life in Ireland when she was braiding my hair. I'll call Tommy in New York." I reached for the phone. "Maybe he can give me more details."

"What would your brother know? She died before he was born."

"But he might have heard her stories secondhand from other relatives." I punched one, two-one-two, then his home number. I heard four rings, then a moment of static and the recording: "This is Tom Gowan. Phone or fax at the tone."

I said, "Hi, it's Margie; call me back," and disconnected.

24

*T*he first call of the morning was from Evaristo, a Cuban who had been my lover some time back. I don't remember exactly when, or for how long, but he was good at it.

"Margo!" He sounded agitated. "I have to show you something. It's about your series on the murdered psychic. Can you meet me for lunch at La Peniche?"

I just grabbed my purse and stopped only to put on lipstick. "Julian, I'm running out to meet Evaristo."

He glanced up from his *Smithsonian* magazine.

"I seem to remember . . . Which one was he?"

"Cuban, black hair . . . Maybe ten years ago."

"Is he plumping for a reprise?"

"No, he sounded scared, not passionate."

At La Peniche, we had the corner table by the window, where Evaristo drummed his fingers on the cloth and lit another Camel.

"I came to you because you are my friend and you are investigating those murders. My uncle, he refuses to tell the police about this."

"Your uncle? I thought all your family was back in Cuba."

"That's so. My mother's brother, Tio Guillermo, lives with his wife

149

outside Havana, but now he is making a three-month visit to our house in East Orleans."

"How nice. I hope Tio Guillermo likes it here."

"No, he does not," Evaristo said firmly. "He says New Orleans is a violent, frightening place and that he has come to appreciate the quiet and safety of Cuba all the more. Today this note came in the mail."

I pushed aside my empty bread pudding dish and took the folded paper from his hand. I didn't need my bifocals. The lettering was eighteen point, and I guessed of the Courier Truetype font: GUILLERMO SANCHEZ! YOU WILL BE THE NEXT PHONY PSYCHIC TO DIE! It was signed with the Ᵽ.

I put the sheet of photocopy paper down flat.

"Is your uncle a phony psychic?"

"Oh, not at all. Tio Guillermo is a priest consecrated to Oggūn."

"Who or what is oo . . . goo . . . ahh . . . ?"

"Oggūn," he pronounced reverently, "is a diety of the Yoruba faith, an old polytheistic religion observed by Afro-Cubans. Oggūn protects all people who work with iron: butchers, farmers, miners . . . "

"But the note calls him a phony psychic. Does your uncle's ministry involve divination at all?"

Evaristo nodded carefully. "When people come to him for help, he throws coconut shells. That's how he understands their problems."

"That makes him fit the profile of 'Pluto's' victims. But your uncle has only been in town two months. And he certainly doesn't advertise. How did the killer learn about him?"

"Don't you read your own paper?"

"That's not in my contract."

"Your features writer, Lillie, did an article about Tio for the Metro section. Here." He opened his briefcase. "I made copies of the page for all our relatives back home."

The article was run alongside a picture of a heavyset mulatto holding a candle.

"This reporter had a fascinating visit with Señor Guillermo Sanchez, an Afro-Cuban priest who is spending his first winter in the Crescent City. Sr. Sanchez, who speaks no English, divined my current status by means of tossed coconut shells. He knew that I was single and the mother of a young son who had recently had health problems . . . "

Evaristo mashed out his cigarette with a vengeance.

"I begged him to let me contact the police about this, but he forbade it. He is sure Oggūn can safeguard him against any evil."

"I seem to recall a young woman called Queen Marie who was just as convinced."

"I know!" Evaristo pulled out a handkerchief and held it against his brow. "I can't convince Guillermo that he should seek protection, so I came to you. But he can't know why."

"That's okay. You can introduce me to your uncle as a troubled person seeking help with a problem."

"Good!" He raised his hand for the check. "We have to stop on the way and buy a bottle of rum."

"Rum? For you or Guillermo?"

"For Oggūn."

Guillermo Sanchez, the third-generation priest of Oggūn, was a portly honey-colored worthy clad in jeans and a startlingly gaudy "Ninja Turtles" T-shirt. But the person was more interesting than his description. He exuded the personal strength and dignity characteristic of all powerful and respected men.

I didn't know whether to curtsy or shake hands, so I settled for a respectful nod. "Good evening, sir."

Evaristo told his houseguest something in Spanish that must have characterized me as a supplicant. The priest nodded and beckoned for us to follow him out to his temporary place of worship, Evaristo's enclosed patio.

There were four votive candles burning in front of a red carpet, on which was exhibited the *nganga,* the shrine to the Yoruban god. The *nganga* was actually a huge iron cauldron filled with beautifully worked artifacts of iron: knives, swords, and crosses. Overhead was a picture of Saint John the Baptist, the Catholic identity of Oggūn.

Guillermo excused himself in Spanish and two minutes later returned wearing a sarong knotted around his waist.

Evaristo handed me the bottle of rum and gestured toward the *nganga.* "Give this to Oggūn."

I stood in front of the cauldron shrine. What does one say to a god one's never met before? Maybe a little flattery was in order.

"Oggūn, I pray you continue to use your great power for good." I placed the bottle of rum in front of the cauldron and backed away with appropriate reverence.

For the divination portion of the service, Guillermo knelt, took a swig of the rum, and spit it out onto the candles—for consumption by the thirsty god.

Guillermo picked four pieces of coconut shell off the carpet, shook them together in his hands like dice, and threw them down on the flag-stones. Then he looked a question at Evaristo, who frowned and shook his head.

"Veo un gran peligro de un hombre muy malo, un asesino!"

I strained to understand. I didn't like that *peligro* thing; it sounded too much like *peril*.

The priest picked up the shells and threw them again. There followed another conference in Spanish amid more mutual headshaking; then Evaristo voiced their conclusion.

"You are in great danger from a man."

"Huh! My life story."

"No, this is very serious, Margo. Guillermo is going to make a charm for you to carry. This will protect you from the evil man."

"Oh, really?" I hope my cynicism didn't stick out too much. "What's it going to set me back?"

"Twenty dollars."

Guillermo nodded in agreement. He understood the number.

"Hey, okay." I dug into my purse. "Salvation for twenty bucks is cheap at the price."

Evaristo and I left the priest to his ritual work and retreated to the kitchen.

Over a cup of too-sweet cocoa, I asked, "No offense, but . . . how can you have a black uncle?"

"He's not black; he's mulatto," Evaristo corrected. "Tío Guillermo is my mother's half brother by grandfather's second wife." He smiled. "In Cuba we are not racist."

152

I smiled back. "Then why were you so emphatic about the distinction between black and mulatto?"

An hour later, Guillermo was ready with the charm, which looked to me like a piece of radish. I was relieved that at least it didn't involve bones or dead animals.

Evaristo listened to his uncle's admonition and translated: "You must not let anybody else see this."

The priest of Oggūn produced a tiny red cotton bag, placed the charm inside, and used a needle and white thread to sew it up.

"If it gets lost," Evaristo cautioned, "don't look for it. That will mean the charm has absorbed the evil and taken it away."

I showed Julian and Gaby the little red bag.

"Evaristo told me his youngest son had asthma so severe he couldn't even play baseball at school. But Guillermo performed a ritual to Oggūn, and the kid hasn't had an attack since. Sounds like he's a pretty powerful god."

"Maybe," Julian conceded. "But if I were looking to serve the most powerful god, I think I'd go sign up with Yahweh. The Jews seem to be accomplishing quite a lot."

Gaby erupted. "Ach"—she waved her hand in front of her face as though shooing gnats away—"I don't believe in any superstition. Christian, Jewish, Pygmy, Hottentot . . . Dey are all primitive nonsense."

The doorbell rang twice briefly, and I sprung up.

"That will be your boyfriend."

It was indeed Brad who stood on the porch holding a loaded grocery bag.

I opened the door wide. "You just went to Schwegmann's?"

"Nope, the food is camouflage," he said, following me into the dining room. "I just went down to the central library." Brad took a clump of celery off the top of his bag and tipped it over. Five books slid out onto the kitchen table.

"This is all they had pertinent to Ireland in the late nineteenth century. That thick one has a good map of Donegal."

Within an hour, we had all made notes of relevant geography, customs, and costumes.

I counted ten pages of loose-leaf, scribbled on both sides. "Now I know where she could plausibly have lived, what she wore, and how she spent her day. But what could she have died of?"

Julian marked a page with a Post-it. "Anyone can die of anything."

"But I'm looking for some nice convenient historical disaster. Trouble is, the Potato Famine was in the 1840s, too early. And the Easter Week Rebellion was 1916. That was too late for her to die young."

"How about the Influenza Epidemic?"

"Did that get to Ireland?" It was too late anyway.

Brad said, "There's always the old standard. Till recent times, more young women died in childbirth than from any other cause."

"I can't use that. There would have been a record and a birth certificate."

"Besides, it's not topical," Julian averred.

Gaby sipped her wine. "But vy all de melodrama of having died tragically?"

"We can't very well say she lived to be eighty-two, can we? For one thing, that would have made it possible for me to know her."

"Right." Julian pulled over a small green volume. "We have to put out that Mavourneen died in Ireland half a world away and half a century before Margo was even born. We want no one to be able to construe a feasible connection."

"Also, old women don't make very attractive spirits," Brad said flatly. "Better to present this one as a fresh, dewy rose of the morn."

*D*id you manage to reach your brother yet?"

"No, Tommy must be out of town. I'll try him again tomorrow." I fell into my wing chair. "What are you watching?"

"Northern Exposure." He held up the remote. "Unless you want to see *Babylon Five.*"

"Lord, no. I just got desensitized to the yucky-looking aliens on *Star Trek* to the point where I actually think Quark is cute. I don't want to have to get used to a whole new set of slimy, oozing monsters."

He turned up the volume. "Look at that Indian woman, Elaine Miles—how she's absolutely untheatrical. Now, either she is the most talented and subtle actress in all of television, or she isn't an actress at all."

"The second one," I said. "She was given the part because she's a genuine Alaskan Indian. So everyone around her acts, and she just sits there and knits . . . " Then came a *doi-oi-oing.* "Hey, Julian! I just thought of a great gimmick for the act. Have you ever seen me knit a sweater?"

He raised an eyebrow. "I've never even seen you *wash* one."

"Neither has anyone else in this town. That's the point. It just occurred to me that a nineteenth-century Irish girl like Mavourneen would know how to knit sweaters in complicated patterns."

"Very likely. But you don't imagine that you can learn the craft in a few days, do you?"

"That's the fun part. Remember, I lived in New York City for two years."

"That dark, degenerate period of your life we'd all like to forget."

"But it wasn't entirely wasted time, Neg. There was a yarn shop on the ground floor of my apartment building, and, well, my days were free . . . "

"Oh, Lordy!" He rolled his eyes to heaven.

"So I took knitting lessons. I'm already an expert."

"An expert?" He snorted with his upper lip, like a horse. "Then how come I never saw you so much as pick up a pair of needles?"

"What would I knit here in New Orleans? An air conditioner? It's a *cold* weather sport."

"That would be a pretty good support for the role you're rehearsing." He nodded thoughtfully. "Margo Fortier can't knit, but Mavourneen Kerrigan can."

I rummaged in the drawer for my tape. "I've got to measure your head."

"You've never taken an interest in my head before."

"So I'll know how big to make the neck. The sweater's going to be for you."

"How thoughtful."

"Trouble is, I can't be seen buying a pattern. Mavourneen wouldn't need one." I rolled back to the phone and dialed. "Hi, Jill? Margo. Tomorrow morning, would you toddle over to that knitting shop on Jackson Square, pick up a pattern for an Irish fishing sweater, and fax it to me?"

"An Irish fishing sweater? Sure, Margo, but . . . since when can you *knit*?"

"Since round about 1890. And don't tell anyone it's for me."

26

*M*y first appearance as a channeler was booked into Sandars Hall, where I was co-billed with The Merry Mix Dance Troop.

My dressing room was a mostly empty storage space with a table and mirror in one corner. I pulled a crate up to the mirror and began an attempt to make myself glamorous, with only a miserable fluorescent light to work by. I hadn't had much practice with theatrical makeup since 1970, and back then, all I had to do was glue on big fluffy lashes and paint around them.

I wet a sponge in a glass of water, rubbed it across the pancake makeup—one shade darker than my skin—and began applying it in upward strokes.

The Sheetrock wall was so thin that I could hear the dancers warming up in their dressing room next door.

"One-two-three-hip, back-two-three-turn . . . "

"Robert? I didn't get my costume!"

"Mack? Where in the name of goodness is Brucie's outfit?"

"There were eight costumes in that box. I hung them up in the corner."

"One-two-turn-kick . . . "

I was clumping on some sable mascara when I heard a two-beat knock on my door and yelled, "I'm not naked!"

"Okay." It was my producer, Andrew, who came in carrying a small, one-foot-square amplifier. "We didn't have a chance to work with this before."

"Work with what?"

"This." From his jacket pocket he produced a microphone and plugged it into a jack in the amplifier.

"They don't have a boom man on duty, so you have to get some facility with a handheld job." He pointed it at me, and I backed away as though from a snake. "Here, Margo. You'll get used to it."

Timorously, I took the thing from his hand and pointed it at the ceiling while he plugged the amplifier cord into the wall socket.

"Not that way. You have to hold it straight out, about two inches from your lips."

"But I don't . . . " I pointed the mike at him and a high *scree* came out of the amplifier.

"No!" He jumped over it and took the mike from my hand. The noise stopped. "That's what we call feedback. Always keep the mike behind the amplifier, and make sure you don't point it anywhere in that direction. You listen to the monitor to make sure you're not too close or too far from the mike. Now let's have a sound check. Speak into it."

"I . . . " I pointed it toward my mouth, like an ice cream cone. "Hello out there . . . " I heard my voice come out of the amplifier and giggled. "Yoo hoo . . . "

Andrew shook his head. "You see why I felt we had to work with this?"

"I'm just nervous."

"For tonight only, I'll pay a guy from the A.V. squad to rig the boom mike so you won't have to think about it. But we won't always have a sound man. You've got to learn how to work with a handheld one."

"Yeah, sure. Right."

As soon as he left, I unplugged the dreadful amplifier and returned to my toilette. I applied a triple thickness of liner that made me look like a raccoon in the mirror but would define my lovely eyes for the rear seats of the auditorium. Then I smeared on a jaw-load of professional-strength rouge.

I could still hear Brucie and his friends through the wall.

"You expect me to go on like *this*?"

"One-two-bump-kick . . ."

Once painted, powdered, and pulled together, I was too nervous to remain in my "dressing room," so wandered backstage and waited in the wings while the Merry Mix Dance Troop cavorted through their routine. The leader did some complicated tap thing in a tailcoat and pants that showed his ankles, while his colleagues waved and kicked behind him in purple tights. I ducked out of the way as the chorus line cha-cha'd offstage and gave my hair one last brush during my introduction.

Andrew held his arms out.

"Ladies and gentlemen, the Mystic Margo has been visited by the spirit of a soul who has passed over, an Irish girl who lived in the last century."

As the audience whispered and mumbled instead of applauding, I glided onstage with my knitting bag over my arm and sat in that same throne chair last occupied by the late Mystic Sydney.

"Her name was Mavourneen Rose Kerrigan," Andrew announced. "She was born in a thatched hut in County Donegal in 1868, and she died tragically from a fall from her horse in 1887. A young girl deprived of her life before she even became a woman."

He had their attention now. They slid forward in their seats, one and all.

"And now the Mystic Margo is going to go into a trance and allow her body to be used by the spirit of this young woman who lived on the west coast of Ireland in the last century."

I closed my eyes and sang Granny Armaugh's favorite verse:

> *"Má faimse slante, is fada a beas tract ir,*
> *an meid is bathu i Anachcuain.*
> *Mo trua amaireac, gach athair is maithir,*
> *bean is paiste ata ag sileath deor."*

(I could not have translated the lines but neither could anyone else in the building.)

Then I looked up with what I hoped was a wholesome, naive expression. I raised my voice to a higher pitch, because after all, I was supposed to be a *young,* rural colleen.

"Ooh, whar is this place? Sure an' Oi've never sayn so many payple in me loife."

I glanced down at Julian in the first row, who put his thumb and forefinger in a circle against his cheek. So the brogue, at least, was sounding okay. I opened my knitting bag, pulled out my needles, and started on a cable-stitched sleeve.

Andrew stayed at his microphone, stage right, and played the part of the interviewer.

"Good evening, Mavourneen. You're in the city of New Orleans, and all these people have come to see you."

"Aye! Bless me!"

"How is your time in the spirit world?"

" 'Tis lovely, so grayn and payceful, with faylds of flowers, sunshoine, an' rainbows—" I stopped short. Julian's two fingers had made a subtle scissoring motion. ("Cut the crap.")

Andrew waved at the audience. "Do you have anything to tell us here?"

"Aye," I twittered. "First Oi have a message for a young woman in this audience. She is thinkin' about a young man. Oi can see that he has a tattoo, a tattoo of blue wroitin', not script, moind you, but printed letters." I waved my arms mystically. "Ye must stay away from him, me dear. The boy is no good for ye. No good a'tall."

A murmur went through the audience. There must have been a dozen girls who thought the message was directed at them, and it was. (Any tattoo of blue printed letters was most likely administered with a needle and ballpoint pen ink to alleviate boredom in a prison cell.)

"Mavourneen?" A hand was raised.

"Yes?" Andrew pointed. "That gentleman with the gray hair."

"Excuse me, I have a question." The man stood up.

"Oi see yer trouble." I waved my hands in front of me. "Ye have just lost yer job in an office. An accounting office. An' yer very upset abaut it."

"That's *right*. How did you know?"

"But wait! Ye have a cousin whose initials are W. T."

"Why, yes, that would be William Tierney."

"He can foile papers ta get yer job back."

"How'd you know? Will is a lawyer, and he handles age discrimination suits! That's amazing!"

Gasps and whispers rustled through the audience as the gray-haired man resumed his seat, shaking his head in wonderment.

"Now I see that a lady in the third row has a question," Andrew proclaimed.

"Hey, Mavourneen? Are you listenin' up theah?" Up bounced the earnest slum lady. "It's me, Jane Bittnah!"

(Oh, Lordy!)

"I was talkin' ta Madame Delphine, las' week, 'bout buyin' proppity ina nint' ward, an' she tole me I should ax my brothah Carl." She slapped her sides bewilderedly. "On'y Carl sez he don't know nuthin' 'bout it."

"Ah, yes," I trilled. "Carl is a foine, earnest lad."

" 'Cept when he drinks!"

"But he has a good heart."

"Yeah?" I could hear the snort all the way up on the stage. "I nevah seen it."

"Yer dayr brother should come back t' Holy Mother Church. Then his breast would be filled with the Lord's blessin's again."

(This was getting to be a strain.)

"Okay, yeah. Now 'bout my real estate problem—"

"Oh, sure an' begorra! Oim in communion with the Doivoine and He gave me the answer t'yer concern." I touched my brow. "Our Lord says all ye nayd do is live in that apartment yerself for six months after ye buy it, then ye'll absorb all the mystical understandin' ye nayd ta deal with the zonin' ordinances."

"Live innit? That rat trap? No! I mean, I jus' wannit ta *rent*!"

Her protest was drowned out by applause, and with visible reluctance, she resumed her seat.

Andrew acknowledged another fluttering white hand.

"Mavourneen, I've been married five years, and we have two children."

"Praise be."

"But now I think my marriage is over."

"That would be sad. Whoi do ye think so?"

Oh, damn! I dropped a stitch. And I couldn't very well interrupt the act to fish around for my crochet needle and pick it up again. On the other hand, it wouldn't have been in character to keep right on knitting, either.

"My husband doesn't care about me anymore. He just comes home from work and heads straight for the TV."

"But he *does* come home from work, ye say." I folded the needles together and put them in my lap, as though betaken by this woman's problem. "He does work, an' he does come home."

"Well, yes. But he isn't romantic anymore."

"Me dayr choild, romance is only a trick nature plays on us so we'll get married an' have babies. 'Tis of no use a'tall afterward."

"But how can I stay with a man who doesn't show he loves me?"

"Faith, but he *does* show he loves ye, by takin' care of yerself an' the children. Sure an' the dayds spayk louder than the words."

"I guess I didn't think of it that way."

"Count yer blessin's dayr. In Oireland, half the women Oi knew were married ta drunks or layabouts, but they just offered it up an' went on with their business. We had a sayin' 'Better the divil ye know!' "

"Mavourneen?" The next voice was that of a young girl, so plaintive and vulnerable that I had to peek through my hands. She looked about sixteen and would have been pretty if she weren't so miserable.

"Yes? What is't, me little colleen?"

"I'm pregnant."

(Oh, Jeez!)

I couldn't see the tears in her eyes, but they were in her voice. "I don't want to have an abortion, but I don't know what else to do."

(How'd I get into this?) I drew in a breath and set my mouth back on the brogue.

"Ah, me darlin', 'tis a great sin ta kill a wee babe in the womb. And

162

'tis a great wrong too ta bring a helpless choild into a world not fit for it."

"So?" She was sobbing aloud now. "What should I do?"

"God is tellin' ye what ta do roight now." I squinched up my face as though listening to some invisible deity. "He says ye must follow yer heart."

Then there was a sigh from the girl, deep and cleansing, as though a great burden had been lifted.

"Thank you, Mavourneen! Thank you!"

(What the hell'd I say?)

After my last bow, Julian met me in the wings.

"It absolutely worked. When Brad stood up and you pretended to read his mind about some job he'd lost, the audience thought you were a miracle worker!"

"Brad did very well for a guy with no theatrical training."

"He didn't need a script. All he had to do was agree with anything you said."

Julian cocked his head, "Say, Margo? What would you do if an adolescent daughter of yours turned up pregnant?"

We stepped over a mike cable. "You know very well what I'd do. I'd have her uptown to the clinic and *unpregnant* before she could spit."

"Then what was all that folderol about"—he twisted up his face in imitation—" 'the great sin of killing a wee babe'?"

"That was Mavourneen's answer, not Margo's. I had to stay in character, didn't I?"

"Interesting." He rubbed his chin meditatively. "Did you ever stop to think Mavourneen might have some insight that you lack?"

"Fat chance."

"Also, I noticed that you're advising all the discontented *housefraus* to stick it out with their husbands."

"They'd better get wise to the fact that it's not a husband's job to keep his wife in a state of constant thrill. Besides, there's no divorce in Mavourneen's world."

"That's because they have no choice in Ireland. Here where we have a choice, it's what? Fifty percent?"

163

"It's all the fault of airheaded soap operas and sappy movies. These days, American girls expect to get an enchanting lover and a responsible husband all wrapped up together in the same man!"

"You don't think that possible?"

"Make sense. They're two different kinds of guys. Good lovers are exciting and erratic and throw their money around. Good husbands, by contrast, are economical, dull, and reliable."

"Like me?"

"Not necessarily *that* dull. A husband has to be good-looking because you're always being photographed with him at family reunions."

"I'm glad it isn't for nothing that I'm good-looking."

"On the other hand, it doesn't matter what a *lover* looks like, because you're going to be meeting him in dark alleys and dimly lit hot-sheet motels along Airline Highway."

"Always the romantic, Margo. By the way, I approve of your answer to the slum queen. That was cute of you to suggest that she go live in one of her own slums."

"There *was* something Solomonic about it."

"But did you have to say 'sure an' begorra'?"

Back in my so-called dressing room, I glopped on some face cream and wiped off the clown-strength makeup. My skin underneath was already pink and bumpy from some allergic reaction. I was losing my enthusiasm for show business.

I opened my purse and rummaged for my Fantasy Rose lipstick, groping unsuccessfully until I finally resorted to dumping the contents onto the floor. I got down on all fours and groveled around, pawing through the makeup, keys, loose change, and candy wrappers until my eye fell on a little red bag. Then I remembered about Guillermo's charm. I picked it up and slipped it into my bra for maximum protection, in the spirit of the old woman who suggested chicken soup for a dead man: "It ken't hoit."

In that second, I got the idea to practice more of my "microphone technique."

I pushed the amplifier over to face the curtainless window then, standing a foot behind it, gingerly pushed the "On" switch, held the mike to my lips, and spoke softly.

"Testing one-two-three-four" came out of my mouth and out of the amplifier and hit the back wall.

Maybe "Testing . . . etc." wasn't a sufficiently challenging speech. I put the mike down on the chair and cast around for something more interesting to recite. A newspaper was rolled up in the wastebasket by the door, so I shamelessly fished it out and carried it back to my broadcast station.

Then the door opened behind me. I turned and saw that it was just one of the Merry Mix dancers, still in his purple tights. I smiled and put my hand up to wave him over to the big dressing room next door.

Then I saw that he was wearing gloves. Then I recognized his eyes. I backed away and drew in a breath to scream, but he had lunged forward and his hands were at my throat before I could let it out.

It's been eighteen years since Coach Hayashi's self-defense class at Tulane, but I retained a single basic maneuver. Without actually thinking about it, I clasped my hands in a double fist and shot them up, punching hard toward the ceiling. Though the attacker was much stronger than I, my biceps were stronger than his thumbs and better leveraged, so I broke his grip, startling him. I'd guess he was used to most people he strangled just clutching futilely at his gloved hands till they passed out. I pulled in another breath as my hands unfisted and clawed his face on the way down. Four fingers connected and scraped red trails in his unprotected face. He grabbed my right hand and twisted it down so hard that I fell in that direction. The live mike was still on my chair, and on my way down, I managed to snatch it by the cable with my left hand and swing it out over the front of the amplifier. The resulting feedback was the most God-awful screech this side of hell, bouncing off all four bare walls. The guy in purple tights let go of me, clapped his hands over his ears, and backed away from the high-pitched noise, too rattled to figure out that he could end it by simply tracing the cable to the plug and yanking it out of the socket.

In the lower-tone range, I heard running footsteps in the hallway. The door was jerked open, and there stood a startled security guard. My assailant whirled around and knocked him flat on his way down the hall and out the open window at the end of it. I kicked my shoes off and ran down the hall after him, to see him scramble over the roof and out of sight. Meanwhile, a crowd had piled up behind me, reacting to the amplifier noise like the extras in a Godzilla movie.

"What the hell?!" The guard was grappling at his holster and nearly knocked me down as I threaded through the crowd on my way back into the room. Trying to cover both ears with one arm, I yanked out the cord to the amplifier, and the unearthly screech stopped.

When I turned around, Frank was in the room with his hand on his holster. "Oh, God, Margo!"

"No problem," I hastened to assure. "Hubie Nadler tried again, but he missed again. I'm okay."

"We had security guards all over the place. I thought no one could get backstage."

"We didn't get here till late in the day." The chief of security was all explanations and apologies. "The assailant must have snuck in early and stolen one of the costumes from the dancers."

"Brucie's costume," I supplied. "That's why he had to dance in an ill-fitting monkey suit and didn't match the others."

The guard was still explaining.

"Whoever it was must have waited till Mrs. Fortier finished her show, then came in here after her. If it hadn't been for that feedback noise . . ." He looked at me strangely, probably imagining me dead, then averted his eyes. "He went out the window before I even got a good look at him."

"Of course Nadler would have had his escape route planned. Rotten luck that you can't identify him."

"Don't worry, Frank. The 'unidentifiable' Hubie Nadler will be easier to spot now," I offered with a touch of brag. "He's got some lovely, deep scratches courtesy of *moi*."

27

When I let myself into the house the next afternoon, Julian glanced up from his anthology and looked startled. "Who are you?! Oh, Margo! I didn't even recognize you!"

"Then I was successful. Andrew told me some of the secrets of disguise. First it mustn't *look* like a disguise." I looked in the hall mirror and winced. "It may be as simple as going without makeup, hiding my red hair under this old hat of yours, and wearing something I would never wear."

"I see."

"For example, you know I haven't worn slacks in public in over ten years."

"For which the public is interminably grateful."

"So I stopped by Jill's apartment in the Quarter, and she gave me this old pair, along with this orange sweater she doesn't want anymore. I don't want it, either; I look terrible in orange. And I got these reading glasses on Canal Street."

I pushed them halfway down my nose and peered over the frames.

"What was the occasion for all this camouflage?"

"I was down at O'Flaherty's Pub, absorbing Irish culture."

"That couldn't have taken long."

167

"I got some more material for the act." I admired my anonymous ugliness in the mirror for a moment, then began dismantling the disguise to reemerge as my glamorous true self. First the hat. "Everybody was very nice about it. They gave me some good geographical info on Donegal."

"You were lucky."

"Maybe." I took off the cheap reading glasses and blinked my still-green eyes. "There are three ways to make people inclined to help you. The first is to be pretty, the second to be rich, the third to be poor."

Julian met my eyes in the mirror. "You can access *one* of those approaches," and turned back to his book.

"Tonight, I have to do the invitations for our annual payback party."

"The year went by that fast? Another party time at our throats?"

"I'm a society columnist. It goes with the job."

"But you're bent on inviting everyone we know in town. You never limit the list to those people we actually have to pay back."

"How can you sort them all out?" I went to my desk and waved my date book at him. "Take this example. We owe Mack and Fritzie a dinner, and Bob and Mary Ann owe us a dinner."

"Then why not just call Mack and Fritzie and send them over to Bob and Mary Ann's?"

"It doesn't work that way. Also I want to ask that beautiful school teacher, Mariette Nuñez."

"Schoolteacher and murder suspect, last I heard."

"Yeah, well. Do you know any nice men for her?"

"You mean single and straight? This is New Orleans, dear."

"I'm also inviting Andrew, Nona and Didi, Howie Potts, and everyone connected with the case."

"That should add some spice."

"I wonder if King Cecil would come."

"He's supposed to be in mourning, I should think."

The phone rang. I checked the caller ID and picked it up.

"Hi, Jill."

"Margo, I just saw the promo for today's *Hilary Show*. And it's about you."

"Me?"

"It starts in five minutes. Channel 4."

The TV was on but turned to the wrong channel; it was the man of the house's interminable cartoons. "Julian, give me the remote."

"No!" He clutched it to his bosom. "Bugs and Daffy are doing a soft-shoe. Look, they've got some good moves."

"That's the only dance they *know,* stupid." I wrestled the remote away from him. "They do it all the time. There's a show coming on about me." I punched zero-three on the cable box.

Hilary is New Orleans's answer to Sally Jessy. She began the program, as always, with microphone in hand, a small elevated stage, and a studio audience.

"As promised, this afternoon's program will be devoted to the 'Mavourneen Phenomenon.' "

Hilary is candy-box pretty, with blond hair and big blue eyes. I used to have a Ginny doll that looked like her.

(Ginny had her own wardrobe of pretty dresses in a little steamer trunk, while I made do with dungarees and flannel shirts.)

"The respected society columnist Margo Fortier has lately been giving performances of an unusual nature. She appears to go into a trance and then begins speaking with an Irish brogue and manifesting the personality of a young woman who lived in Donegal before the turn of the century."

"Our first guest is Sigrid Heffernan, who has been Margo Fortier's best friend since college but says there is nothing familiar about this new character who has emerged."

Sigrid, stunningly painted and coiffed by Teri Case for the occasion, acknowledged the polite applause with a forced serious nod.

"Upf! Look at that, Julian. *She's* not my best friend. I can't stand that harpy."

"We can assume that she only said she was your best friend to get on Hilary's show. I know a fellow who claimed to be a *drag queen* just to get on Hilary's show. First time he ever wore a dress in his life was on the air."

"That's different."

169

"His parishioners were in shock."

"Some people crave attention at any price, but it's pretty pathetic to claim a relationship that doesn't exist."

"Just as you claimed to be Delphine's friend to get a byline?"

Hilary went on without us.

"Taking the other side is our second guest, Randall Jooby, the famous magician and debunker. He holds that Margo Fortier is merely playing a part and that Mavourneen Rose Kerrigan is a fraudulent charade."

Jooby rated more applause than Sigrid, which he accepted holding his hands out as though styling after an effect.

"Sigrid," Hilary began, "you believe that Margo Fortier is indeed channeling a departed soul."

"Yes, I do."

"Naive," Jooby muttered.

"No, I'm not naive. In fact, I was skeptical about the whole thing, till I went to see the performance myself and saw her up onstage knitting that beautiful sweater."

Jooby leaned forward. "What's so hard about that?"

"Nothing if you know how," Sigrid retorted. "But everyone knows Margo Fortier can't knit."

"What makes you so sure?" Jooby pressed on. "Did it ever come up in conversation prior to this charade? Did you ever hear her say 'too bad I can't knit,' or something to that effect?"

"No, but I've known her nearly twenty years, and I've never seen her do it."

"No one has seen me ride a bicycle in the past twenty years, either. But I assure you that I can if I want to."

The response to that was scattered laughter and then a commercial.

The beautician John Jay's spot featured a makeover in split screen. As usual, the subject had looked younger and prettier "before" Jay's scissors-mad gremlins sheared the poor trusting soul down to the earlobes. I'm convinced that most hairdressers hate hair.

When the show came back on, Hilary consulted a card then put out a question.

"Some members of our audience have called in to say Mrs. Fortier was singing in the Gaelic language during her appearance as Mavourneen. Do you have any comment on that?"

"More proof!" Sigrid crowed. "Margo has never been in Ireland. Where would she learn any Gaelic?"

"Who says it's Gaelic?!" Jooby thundered. "There was no one in the audience who understands the language. She could have been speaking in *tongues* for all anyone knows!"

"Uh-oh, I see a problem," Julian muttered. "Margo, what Gaelic do you know besides that verse?"

I shrugged. "Just *Erin go bragh* and *Slanté.* But I guess I can fake it."

"Fake it? Lord!" Julian clapped his hands over his ears. "Don't even try! There may be only three people in the whole region who can actually understand Gaelic, but you can bet that they will all be front row center at your next performance, compliments of your friend Randall Jooby. No bluff is feasible."

"Okay then, we'll say Mavourneen was raised in a part of Ireland where Gaelic was no longer spoken by the 1890s. No problem. That's most of the country."

"Oh no, we're cooked! You've already established that this girl grew up in Donegal. They still speak Gaelic over there today! There's no reason why Mavourneen wouldn't have mastered the tongue a hundred years ago."

28

*I*t was the day of the annual pay-back party, and with the worst will in the world, I was doing the wifey-wife thing, cleaning up.

Julian stepped in with his finger in a book.

"Do you have to run that vacuum?"

(If not me, who else? We used to have a saint of a cleaning woman named Effie. But three years ago her six kids chipped in and bought her a little house and an annuity. Now she only does her own housework. We've been afraid to hire another cleaning woman because she'd be liable to steal.)

I shut the vacuum off just long enough to say, "You can't hear it. You're out front painting the iron gate."

"Is that what I'm supposed to be doing? A kid came by looking for work the other day. I should have given him the job."

"Grow up, Neg. That boy wasn't looking for work; he was casing the joint. John and Lucinda let a kid cut their lawn last month, and that very night, their ten-speed bikes were stolen out of their garage."

"What's the world coming to? We have no servant class anymore."

"Forget it. That's been supplanted by the welfare and criminal classes. And right now, it's just you and me." I got down on my knees and looked for dust balls under the bookcase. As always, I wasn't disappointed.

After the first forty minutes of party time, I was just starting to get into the swing of things. King Cecil had found a corner and was keeping the beat with his bongos. Andrew was in deep conversation about the Stanislavski method with Lillie from the paper. Dr. Ingram had come because he was afraid I would spill something about his private life. But he had left Edna home and now stood behind the buffet drinking white wine and looking nervous. Howie Potts was giving Marilou Gendron some instant sun-sign astrology. I drifted through the rooms, getting the usual fragments of party chitchat.

" . . . Say what you want, Soon-Yi *is* of age."

" . . . I could see cheating on Camilla with Diana, but . . . "

"I'd say Mugibur has all the personality. He's *carrying* Sirijul."

" . . . But the big ones don't stay up. You ever seen a Johnny Holmes movie? . . . "

"I just saw a butterfly crawl under the refrigerator . . . "

"Well, hi, Albert." I greeted Julian's barber with a friendly hug. "You're looking trim. You must be on an exercise program."

"Yeah, right. Exercise." But his eyes were old.

"Keep it up!" I chirped, and escaped to the buffet table.

When I run into a friend who has recently lost a lot of weight, I congratulate him on his trim new look, pretending I think it's the result of some health regime.

AIDS used to be topic A at every gathering. "They say Liberace may have it" or "A man in my office is being tested for it." It was always someone "other" who was infected. And weren't we smug and grateful that we weren't like *those* unlucky losers.

But now the gay plague has become so epidemic that nobody mentions it at parties anymore. Because the person you're talking to has it. Or his brother has it, or his best friend just died of it.

As with most middle-aged parties, the gender division takes place long about the third hour. By six o'clock, most of the males had congregated in the kitchen so they wouldn't have to walk too far for their beer, and the women on my personal A-list had crowded into my bedroom for a hen session.

Jill had brought a plate of hors d'oeuvres to the bed, where she rested against the bolster and presented her problem for open debate. "I'm starting to chafe at this celibacy thing after two whole years. So I was just looking around for prospects, right?"

"So what's the problem?" I wondered on behalf of the group.

"The problem is a plausible partner! I met this lawyer last month who looked very possible. I mean, he's sixty years old and very rich, so I figure he could buy me great presents. Right?"

"Theoretically."

"Also, he travels a lot, so he could take me on shopping trips to maybe Hong Kong and Seoul, first class. Add to that, he's well-connected, so he could introduce me to the great and near great, oil moguls and cattle barons. And with all this inventory, do you know what he offered me?"

Gaby shrugged her "I can't imagine" shrug.

"His *body*!" Jill fairly shrieked. "I mean, his sixty-year-old wrinkled, flabby, no-longer-virile *body*!"

"Maybe the old goat thought you wanted sex."

"If all I wanted from a man was sex, I'd get a teenaged boy! That's *their* specialty." She took a toast point with black caviar for instant gratification, in lieu of love and romance. "This is a port town, after all. I could run down to a riverfront bar and scoop up a cute eighteen-year-old Norwegian deck boy who would do anything I wanted as many *times* as I wanted."

In this spirit of self-revelation, Kelley said, "I used to live with a biker named Eugene, and I guess I was very impressionable then. It's been over for years, and I swear I don't have any feeling at all for him. Really. But the trouble is, I still say his name in my sleep." She put her face in her hands. "And I just lost my third boyfriend over this. It doesn't feel great for someone named Robert to hear his girlfriend calling out 'Eugene.' "

Gaby, recumbent on my settee, gestured with the olive from her martini. "You had better bring home a little cat und name it 'Eugene' if you know vat is goot for you."

"I get it! So the guy will think I'm talking about the cat?"

" 'Ach Liebling!' " Gaby struck a wide-eyed pose. " 'But I thought der kitty vas pulling my blanket!' "

"While we're playing 'Dear Gaby,' " said Liz, "I have another problem. My slob of a husband leaves the toilet seat up. I nearly fell in last night."

Kelley held out her Chianti bottle. "Write on the underside in indelible ink, 'If you like to suck dicks, so signify by leaving this up.' "

I said, "That wouldn't work with *my* husband."

A half hour later, the party outside our room was winding down, but we had stocked up on provisions and were still in progress.

Jill drummed her fingers on her now-empty tray.

"James Earl Jones."

"Too easy," I said. "How about Michael Dorn?"

"The Klingon?!"

"But he's *gorgeous* when he's not being a Klingon."

"Okay then," Nona volunteered. "Dorian Harewood."

The bedroom door opened. "Excuse me, ladies?" Julian poked his head in from the hallway. "I couldn't help overhearing, and I'm curious. What is this interchange?"

"It's a game we invented," Kelley said. " 'If we could be black for one Saturday night, whom would we want to spend it with?' "

"Goodness, that sounds like fun. Can I play too?"

"Okay, but it's Gaby's turn."

As Julian closed the door behind him and made himself comfortable on the linen chest, Gaby raised her stem glass. "Harry Belafonte."

"Oh no," Jill grimaced. "You bring him up every time. Belafonte is the old standard. We should retire him to the 'Black for one Saturday Night' Hall of Fame."

"Vell, so is James Earl Jones!"

"Stop bickering girls," Kelley said. "How about Robert De Niro?"

"He's not black."

"But I think he would like me if *I* were."

"I'd take O. J. Simpson."

"Not *him*!"

"Why not?"

"He's so cheap," Kelley said. "He calls his poor old mother *collect,* and she has to jump over all the furniture to answer the phone."

"I'm sure he doesn't. He just wanted to let his mom make a commercial, so he endorsed the service."

"I guess you're right. O.J. wouldn't do that."

"My turn," Julian interposed. "Charles Barkley."

"You nuts? *He's* not gay. He'd kick your impudent butt all over the court."

"As I understand the rules of the game, guaranteed mutual attraction is *not* a prerequisite." He wrinkled his nose. "After all, I don't think Michael Dorn would be interested in Margo, whether black or white, fat or thin, drunk or sober."

"He's got you there, Margo."

By nine o'clock, all the company had taken their leave and shuffled on back to their real lives.

Julian was stacking dishes. "My junior vice president was really smitten with your schoolteacher. He's never seen anyone so beautiful and unspoiled."

"I hope he's good enough for her."

"Here's a nice big ham bone, Catherine." Julian put it in her mouth. "Be sure to drag it all over the floor." He smiled. "I derive a great sense of empowerment from giving a command that's instantly obeyed."

I fell forward across my bed in a graceful sprawl and snoozed for about five minutes before Julian woke me with a clap of his hands.

"Margo? It's nearly nine o'clock." He tugged my foot. "Come on. Help me pack up the stuff."

"Wha-at?"

"Remember, we're going to take this extra food over to the Louis House."

"Can't we wait till tomorrow?"

"You know it never tastes as good the second day."

I propped up on my elbows. "Most of those patients can't taste anything anyway."

"That's why we must try all the harder to bring them something nice. Now, hustle your bustle."

"Oh"—audible groan—"All right."

I rolled off the bed, then trudged into the living room and stood with my hands in front of me, dangling at the wrists like a dog's paws so Julian wouldn't try to put anything in them as he charged around emptying serving bowls into plastic freezer dishes for safe transport.

Out in the car, Julian took the wheel and I sat in the right seat, with the leftover casserole on my lap, not trusting it to the trunk.

"Look at that!" He nodded to the left and gritted his teeth. "Those new neighbors painted their house *lavender*! Right on our own block."

"Disgusting. Isn't that against zoning regulations?"

"It ought to be. This is legally a historic district." He turned right on North Rampart. "How could anyone paint their house *lavender*?"

"Maybe you'll get desensitized."

"I can't wait."

"Visit the sick . . . Bury the dead . . . " are two of the corporal works of mercy observed in spirit when we go to Louis House, where they bury the sick and we visit the dead.

Three years ago, a registered nurse named Jason Vidrine turned his twelve-room family home into a hospice for AIDS patients. It must be a fashionable address; he has never lacked for tenants.

We bring food over whenever we can, as sort of an offering to the monstrous AIDS god. Maybe he'll be pleased with the quiche and broccoli and refrain from invading the bloodstream of Julian or me or any of our close relatives. This year at least.

"Julian, I never know what to tell these people."

"Tell them?"

"Usually, when you see someone who's sick you say 'I hope you get better soon.' But what can we say to someone we're damned certain will *never* get better?"

"We can say, 'I hope you *feel* better.' "

Louis House was behind a little iron gate decorated with ivy. There was nothing to identify the hospice for what it was, just a little sign on the door showing a gun barrel pointed at the visitor: THANK YOU FOR NOT SMOKING.

178

We were both loaded down with freezer dishes, but Julian managed to ring the bell with his elbow. It was Jason himself who opened the door for us. I was glad to see that he was still chubby.

"Oh, the 'fascinating Fortiers'!" He relieved me of an armload. "I'll bet that's more of your delicious gourmet cooking."

We followed him right on through to the spotless kitchen, where four men, three white and one black, sat playing cards.

"More food from the Fortiers," Jason trilled.

"Oh, thank you, Jesus," the black one said. "I'm so tired of my own cooking!"

"Fill your face," Jason invited. "But remember to see me for your shot before bedtime."

We helped dish out the food, then left them to their repast.

"Those are the ones still healthy enough to sit at the table," Jason confided. "The others are bedridden."

I leaned toward him and whispered, "You're injecting these people every day, and cleaning up their blood and bodily fluids. Aren't you afraid you might get infected?"

"I may, but I'm not afraid." He shrugged. "If you do what you believe is right, how can you regret anything that happens to you?"

Julian glanced into a vacant bedroom. "The last time we were here there was a kid named Roger. But he must be gone by now."

"Roger? No, he's still hanging on. I can't imagine how." Jason frowned darkly. "Or why."

"I heard some people stay healthy for ten years after diagnosis. How did Roger get so sick so fast? He's just a kid, not even twenty-five."

"Some strains are more virulent. And different bodies react differently." Jason frowned. "And this boy smoked. The smokers go much quicker."

He led us into the room that looked out over the garden, lit only by one dim bulb. The patient made no move except to breathe, and that was very faint.

"Roger?" Jason said softly. "Do you remember Julian and Margo Fortier?"

"Margo Fortier? Yes." The boy's voice was faint. "I heard about you on television. And Mavourneen . . . Please . . . I'd like to ask her something . . . Mavourneen . . . "

I couldn't lie to these guys. I touched his arm gently.

"Roger, Mavourneen is a stage act. For entertainment purposes only."

"Don't say no." He put out his hand, emaciated and disfigured with purple blotches, and clutched my wrist. "I'm so scared of the end . . . just falling into some big black hole. I have to talk to her. Please?"

Jason, standing behind him, locked eyes with me and nodded. Julian looked away in embarrassment.

"Very well, then." I sat in the armchair at the foot of his bed. "If you'll all be quiet for a minute, I'll try to call up Mavourneen."

I did the act the same as for a paying audience, pretending to come out of a slumber and raising my voice to sound youthful.

"Hello? Who is here callin' me?"

"It's me. Over here!" Roger looked eager, like a child in a wasted, wizened body. "Mavourneen? Tell me . . . What is going to happen to me? After? . . . "

"After?" I made out that I was cogitating. "Why, sure an' ye'll be floatin' right up hayr ta Heaven. An', ah, 'tis the most beautiful state, only the koindest God could have made for us." It was pure improvisation. "With the softest colors an' the swaytest music. An' there's ought but love up hayr for those who carry it in their hearts."

"Will my . . . my mother be there when I come?"

"Oh yes. She's watchin' ye now from above. She tells me she misses her boy greatly."

"Oh, Mommy!" His eyes were closed, but tears slid down his hollow cheeks. "I thought you *hated* me!"

"She says she's so sorry for wastin' the chance ta tell ye how precious ye were ta her whoile she was aloive."

"She wouldn't see me. She never even answered my letters."

I got so angry at the bitch it was difficult to stay in character. But for the kid's sake, I stifled my feelings and kept my voice even.

"Yer mother was very confused about the road yer loife had taken. But once she got hayr ta Heaven, she came ta understand yer good heart. An' now she wants me ta tell ye that right this minute she fayls the most proide that any woman can ever fayl for her son."

"She's proud of me now?"

"The minute ye cross over, though, the first soul ta grayt ye will be a man. He loves ye very much." Jason nodded vigorously. "He's tryin' ta tell me his name now. It's . . . " Jason mouthed something, but I couldn't read his lips. "Spell it out fer me; it's . . . " Then Jason turned around and wrote the name in the air. I repeated the letters as he made them. "G-O-R-D-O-N."

"It's Gordon?"

"Aye, that's the young man. Oi see him now. He . . . " Jason held one hand high over his head, then rubbed his chin. "He's tall an' has a beard."

Roger was too tired to open his eyes again but smiled weakly. "Yes. Gordon had the softest red beard."

"That he does. An' . . . " Jason cocked his left arm and with his right hand described a bulging bicep. "Ah, the muscles on him."

"He's got his muscles back in Heaven? Oh, thank God! He was so thin before he died."

"An' he's tellin' me that ye mustn't be afraid. Now he's laughin'. He says there are . . . What's that, Gordon? I don't understand the words. 'There are no fag-bashers in Heaven.' "

The patient laughed feebly, a whispered "Uh-huh."

"Gordon always had wit, you know," he added.

"An' now he's holdin' his arms out ta ye, just waitin' fer ye ta layve yer poor, sick body behind an' go mayt him."

"I'm coming, Gordon." The ruin of a young man smiled contentedly. "It won't be long now, I know."

Jason nodded, and I pretended to come out of the trance.

"What? . . . What happened?"

Julian looked out the window. "You should have been here."

"It was real . . . It had to be." Roger clutched for Jason's arm. "She even knew all about Gordon. I never told her that."

"No, you never did."

"He's waiting for me. We'll be together again."

We kissed Roger good-bye, then Jason walked out between us, his arms around our shoulders.

"Thank you so much. He needed to hear all that."

Julian didn't speak till we were out on the sidewalk.

"Congratulations. That was the first time your Mavourneen act actually did some good."

"Fat chance Roger's crud of a mother is in Heaven."

"You told him the right thing, though. The comforting thing. Every boy wants to believe his mother loves him."

Back in the car, I leaned my head against the window.

"The kid is only twenty-four years old. How many times could he have had intercourse in his young life, and he has to die for it. When I was twenty-four, I was . . . "

Julian started the engine and activated the wipers to remove condensation. "Let's not hear what *you* were doing, Margo."

"But we were *all* doing it back then. Someone's cute? Fine. You go to bed with him. If there's no magic with him, tomorrow night, someone else will be cute. No problem."

He shook his head. "Our generation was so spoiled. We thought we were entitled to sexual license."

"It was the natural thing."

"Not so natural, dear. Consider that throughout most of history, sex had been a dangerous undertaking."

"I never considered that."

"Syphilis and gonorrhea were incurable and deadly. Contraception wasn't available. Childbirth was often fatal, abortions even more often. If a woman bore a child out of wedlock, both lives could be ruined." He pursed his lips. "*My* kind were ostracized, imprisoned, or stoned to death in the name of God."

"Abominable."

"So in all of human history, there were only about fifteen years, from 1965 to 1980, when the masses could practice promiscuity with few physical or social consequences."

"What does all that mean?"

"Has it occurred to you that maybe Mother Nature just plain doesn't like free sex?"

"So now that it's fatal again . . . "

"Mother Nature must be happy as a pig in slop."

Catherine was in the front yard as we drove up and stood there barking in staccato yelps for all she was worth.

Julian parked in a neat parallel to the curb and called, "What's all the commotion about, Catherine? Did you miss us that much?"

"I doubt it. Did you forget to feed her?"

"That can't be her issue. Remember, she got everybody's scraps from the party."

I was first out of the car and up the front steps.

"Hey, Julian! Something smells like gas." I unlocked the front door.

"Gas?" He ran up the steps behind me. "Where is it coming from?"

"Inside the house, I think." I reached out. "Eeyoww!"

That last remark was a reaction to Julian's jerking me violently backward. We landed together in a tangled heap on the porch. I flailed arms and legs like a bug on its back.

"What did you do *that* for?!"

"Huh?"

He was perfectly calm, as though he hadn't been unspeakably rude. "You were reaching for the light switch, weren't you?"

"Well, of course. We have to see inside. What's wrong with that?"

"The light switch makes a spark."

I arose gracefully, first rolling off him, then turning over on all fours and hoisting myself up with a grunt.

"No, it doesn't."

"Yes, it does." He leapt to his feet and brushed off his coat. "A teeny one inside the wall. But it's a big enough spark to ignite a houseful of gas and blow the place to smithereens, and we would die here like idiots because you"—here he mimicked me, raising the pitch of his voice and affecting my nasal New Jersey accent—" 'Just had to seee insiide.' "

"Okay," I begrudged. "One little mistake."

"Now, Margo"—he held me by the shoulders—"I'm running to the car for the flashlight. You just stand stock-still and don't move a finger."

Julian took only a moment to retrieve the flashlight. Then he turned it on and grabbed a deep breath before making his dash through the house. I listened to his progress as he hit every room on the first floor, opening all the windows. He was back in less than a minute.

"I put the fans blowing through the back door. We'll wait out here till the gas dissipates." He settled on the stone bench with a sigh. "I checked all the gas jets. It was the floor heater in the guest room. The handle was turned just a fraction, so we had a slow leak. It had to take hours to fill up the house."

"How could that heater have been on? We haven't used the guest room in days."

"Maybe you jiggled it while vacuuming."

"Vacuumed a room no one was expected to enter?"

"Of course not. What could I have been thinking?"

"I can't imagine. The last time I vacuumed that room was when your Aunt Lisette came to visit."

"Aunt Lisette died in '87."

"I know."

"And she was bedridden in Shreveport five years before that."

"Yes."

"Funny, though. It had to have happened today, during the party. Maybe one of our guests—"

"Wandered into that room and turned the heater on? What for? It was seventy-two degrees out this afternoon."

"Then it must have been done accidently."

"You know what? If we hadn't gone out to Louis House, we would have just fallen asleep in there and woke up dead."

"Good deeds are sometimes rewarded."

*R*ound about six-thirty Monday evening, Officer Gendron left me in front of police headquarters on Broad Street, and I found my own way back up to Frank's office. He and Duffy were sorting through photographs.

"Yoo hoo! Do you have more pictures of Nadler for me to look at?"

"Not necessary, Margo. Your pal was just found in a motel room up in La Place." He grinned. "With his brains all in disarray."

He straightened a handful of file cards and hummed a strain of "It's a grand night for singing."

"Neat!" I moved a stack of folders from a chair to the floor and took its place. "Much as I like Marilou, I'm relieved not to need a bodyguard anymore. Do they know what time it happened?"

"They've got it pretty close. Nadler was seen eating fried chicken in the adjacent diner at six o'clock. An analysis of the stomach contents puts his death not later than six-thirty."

"Neat! Who gets the credit for doing him?"

"It may be that Nadler can take the bow himself." Frank chuckled. "The gun was found near his right hand, and there was no sign of an intruder. The physical evidence seems to indicate suicide."

"Cruds like Nadler don't kill themselves. What on earth for? Remorse? He was a *sociopath*!"

"It doesn't gibe with my conception of him, either, but here's another item of interest. Delphine's ring was in his pocket. The one she wore on all the commercials."

"Then Nadler must have killed Delphine. You can clear the case."

He nodded. "So that would seem to be that. Except . . . " Frank slapped the file. "Nadler never used a sword in any of his hits. Not once. Why would he change M.O.s for Delphine?"

"Her saber was close to hand?"

"His gun was closer. No." Frank spread his fingers over the file, as though trying to read it in braille. "That sword was wielded by an expert, and there's no indication that Nadler ever fenced in his life."

"Maybe in school?"

"His school was Parchman Prison, and no, they didn't have a fencing team."

"How about this?" Duffy intervened. "What if Nadler just didn't want to use his own gun, because it was subject to a ballistics match, and as for that clean stroke to the heart"—he shrugged—"lucky strike. What does Margo think?"

I moved my head negatively. "No connection to Pluto."

"Aw, Frank, is she gonna start that stuff again?"

"Calm down, Duffy. That's why she's here."

"You never did explain that move. Why *is* she here?"

Frank patted his file. "I read that Winston Churchill used astrologers. Of course, he didn't believe in them for a minute, but he knew that *Hitler* did." He pointed. "Margo is helping us to elicit what Delphine had in mind, see?"

I said, "I can tell you about Delphine's frame of reference. But what did *Nadler* have in mind? What could have been his motive for killing a phony psychic?"

"For simple profit." Duffy leaned forward with his fists on his hips. "To steal that fancy ring."

"Then why hadn't he turned it into money?"

"I hate questions like that." He slapped the desk in front of Frank. "But if Nadler didn't off himself, who would have?"

"Anyone. *I* would have." Frank admitted. "The real question is, whom would Nadler allow to get close enough to kill him?"

"Only a friend," I said.

"If he had any friend at all, it was only one."

Duffy jabbed a finger. "That would be the guy who killed him."

*T*hank you for agreeing to see me." I smiled, and I hoped it looked
real.

"Any time." Jooby's return smile looked phonier than mine. "Nice little coffee shop."

"Lovely." I pulled Nona's photocopy out of my purse and pushed it
across the table. "I'd like to have a chat about this."

He adjusted his glasses and read the paper, then folded his arms. "Go
ahead."

"Would you like to explain Delphine's check written to and endorsed
by you for five thousand smackers?"

He grinned instantaneously, like a twitch. "No problem. It was a consulting fee."

"What would a phony psychic consult you about?"

"Her stage show. She wanted to use some new effects."

"Wowee. So the world's greatest debunker was going to help a phony
psychic fool the public."

"Not at all." He swept his hands out gracefully. "Delphine—Miss
Harris—had given me her word that she would cease to represent her
demonstrations as paranormal. She was designing a new act as an honest stage magician."

"How all-of-a-sudden enlightened of her. And wouldn't you know, she had to go and get herself murdered before telling another soul of her virtuous intentions."

"Exactly. And I was as shocked as you were."

"Mrs. Fortier!"

A fleshy woman I'd never seen before in my life had just popped out of the ladies' room. She heave-hoed up to our table and, ignoring Jooby, loomed over me and clutched my hand. "Mrs. Fortier! Oh, I have so much to thank Mavourneen for."

"I . . . beg your pardon? . . . "

"You— That is, Mavourneen told my daughter to stop seeing that terrible ex-convict."

"I'm sure she didn't specifically—"

"Oh yes, remember? You warned her about the tattoo."

"The tattoo? Ah . . . blue printed letters . . . "

"Yes, on his right arm: 'Born to be bad.' Just like you said. Well, I managed to get her to stay home last night, and while she was watching television"—she whooped with glee—"Jeff actually got arrested for possession! Just as you told us."

I accepted the woman's thanks, declined her kind offer to pay for my hot chocolate, and sent her on her way.

Prediction is easy. You give someone a word, and she'll obligingly elaborate it into a sentence, a paragraph, even a story, which she will then twist and squeeze to fit her own circumstances.

Jooby watched my fan toddle out the door before making comment. "Now for my side of the chat." His eyes glittered behind his sunglasses. "I was curious about Mavourneen Rose Kerrigan. The details you gave your audience about her life are uncanny."

I put my fingers to my head. "They just came to me."

"Sure they did. It happens that I have a friend in Ireland who owed me a favor. I asked him to do some research for me."

I smiled brightly. "And did he?"

"He just faxed me the information. The town is exactly as you describe, and everything you've been saying about nineteenth-century Donegal, from customs to costumes, is absolutely authentic for the time."

"Naturally."

"My contact searched through county records of the last century for the name Mavourneen Rose Kerrigan and found out there *was* a girl of that name born in Donegal in July of 1868."

"July eighteenth," I said.

His eyes widened. "Yes, exactly."

I tapped my brow.

"And she was baptized in St. Brigit's Parish Church four weeks later. But there is no further mention of her in the records or newspapers that have been preserved from the time. She must have lived a quiet life. So far as we can determine, there was never any note taken of her in that record archive in Donegal but her birth and baptism."

"That's not unusual, is it?" I asked demurely. "During that era, a proper lady's name would appear in the paper only three times: at her birth, at her marriage, and at her death."

"Right. So I've got one. Where are two and three? I admit to reaching a dead end." He frowned. "For the time being, anyway. I understand that you've never been to Ireland, much less Donegal."

"Never been to Europe, much less Ireland."

"So, how could you have known anything about Mavourneen Rose Kerrigan?"

"I don't know." I held my palms out like a Fugawe Indian. "This ability I have is just—"

"No!" He pulled over the ashtray. "That's bullshit. There's a natural explanation for all this, and I'm going to find it." He opened a box of brown cigarettes. "I did get far enough to figure out where you got the idea for this character."

"Oh?"

"You and I are both old enough to remember *The Search For Bridey Murphy.*"

"Not much." I scratched my head and squinted. "I seem to recall that it was a book."

"Top of the best-seller list in 1956."

"What do you want? I was only eleven."

"It was the story of this Colorado housewife." Jooby lit a cigarette and took one long drag. "A Mrs. Virginia Tighe. She had a neighbor, a salesman named Morey Bernstein who fancied himself an amateur hypnotist. He put the woman under 'hypnosis' . . . " Jooby made the quotation marks with his fingers. "Mrs. Tighe was supposedly in a trance when she started speaking with a brogue and claimed to be the reincarnated soul of an Irish girl from Cork, one Bridey Murphy."

"I vaguely remember the story."

"Mrs. Tighe recounted her anterior life in great detail. She told all about Bridey's metal bed, her wooden house, and her husband who taught law at Queen's University. It all seemed very plausible at the time, and the whole country became reincarnation crazy. They marketed a film about Bridey Murphy, TV shows, records, even popular songs."

"It's all hazy now."

"Sure, because the phenomenon"—he snapped his fingers and made a *pff* sound—"dried up and blew away when researchers couldn't substantiate the account. They found no record of the people or the streets Mrs. Tighe described. Even the wooden house and metal bed were unlikely for the time and place."

"So she was a phony. But how, incidentally, did they explain her detailed recollections?"

"Elementary. The woman had grown up around Irish immigrants, one of whom even had the maiden name Bridey Murphy."

"That's shocking."

"So, naturally that led me to you. You're Irish, right?"

I couldn't very well deny it with *this* face.

"My maiden name is Gowan."

"I know. So you could have had contact with someone like Mavourneen when you were a little girl. A friend of the family maybe, even a relative."

"It's certainly possible." I made my eyes big and round. "But I don't remember."

"I'll *help* you remember," he said with an insinuation of threat. "By the way, where are you from?"

"Boonton, New Jersey."

"An Irish neighborhood?"

"Mostly Polish-Italian."

191

"I'll look into it. See what I can find."

"Great." I did a perky smile. "Let me know."

Julian clapped his brow. "Oh, Lord. He's going to trace Mavourneen Rose Kerrigan all the way to Ellis Island and find out she's your great-grandmother and your pitch will be queered."

"That can't happen," I assured. "When Granny was twenty-three, she went to visit a second cousin in Killarney. That's all the way down at the other end of the country. She met Brendon Armaugh at Sunday mass and married him in the same church. And it was as Mavourneen Armaugh that she immigrated to the U.S. in 1894. See? There's no record that Mavourneen Rose Kerrigan ever existed after her baptism."

"Then we can only hope he doesn't have the good sense to work backward."

"Backward?"

"Now that he's lost the trail of Mavourneen, it's not likely he'll ever find out how she leads to you. So next he should research *your* early life and study any connections *you* might have had to *her*."

"That seems to be his plan. He just asked me about my hometown."

Julian shook his head. "Damn, he's getting awfully close."

"Let Jooby knock himself out. Do you think anyone is still alive in Boonton to remember an octogenarian who died in 1950?"

"Don't bet it can't happen. There are a lot of old women sitting on porches who have nothing better to do than to remember. And they discuss their memories with anyone who'll take the time to sit on the porch with them."

"If they do, they'd only remember a Granny Armaugh, not Mavourneen Rose Kerrigan."

"In any event, written records don't forget."

"Don't sweat the paper trail, Neg. My mom was born in Newark in 1925. *Her* mom was born in rural Kansas in 1906. Let him hunt up *that* birth certificate. Anyhow, Jooby only has to chase his tail long enough for me to find out if it was really Nadler who killed Delphine. Then I'll drop the act."

"You think he'll stop trying to expose you then?"

"The question will be moot. Old news. And by that time, we won't care. They sure can't indict me as a swindler. We haven't taken any money from anyone, and we present the act 'for entertainment purposes only.'

The phone trilled, and I picked it up. "It's your nickel."

"Margo?" It was Jason from Louis House.

"Sure, hi."

"I just want to tell you, Roger died last night."

"Oh?"

"I sat with him and held his hand till the end. He was smiling. He wasn't afraid anymore, thanks to you."

And there was a tall man named Gordon with a red beard waiting for him when he crossed over. I know it.

"Thank you" was all I had to say, and we disconnected.

Julian looked a question.

"It was Jason," I said. "Roger finally passed away."

"Good."

"Yes, it's good. He's at peace now but . . . "

"But what?"

"He missed Christmas."

32

I was in conference with Andrew in his Dauphine Street apartment when Frank Washington knocked on the door.

"Margo? What are you doing here?"

"Planning our next show. You?"

"I've come to talk to Mr. Berry."

"Welcome," Andrew called jovially. "Grab yourself a chair."

"Thank you." Frank took the closest seat and started the interview on a high note. "We have some news for you, Mr. Berry. We've discovered the body of a man named Hubie Nadler, a suspected murderer."

"I heard all about it on the news. Self-induced capital punishment. I'm all for it."

"We're not yet sure it was self-induced." Frank reached into his pocket and brought out a plastic bag with the sapphire ring. "Do you recognize this?"

Andrew wasn't invited to handle the bag, so just nodded.

"I'd know it anywhere. It has to be Frieda's ring. She said it was one of a kind."

"Since this ring implicates Nadler in your employer's death, we have to consider that you had a motive to kill him."

"Better than anyone's," Andrew admitted. "Even if Delphine weren't a personal friend, I still can't see making a living without her."

"The M.E. reports the time of Nadler's death as between six and seven o'clock. Do you remember where you were during that hour?"

Andrew shrugged. "The same as every night when we're not doing a show. I was right here, sitting in that rocking chair, reading a book . . . No, a magazine. Probably *Newsweek*."

"Did anyone call you or drop by?"

"No one. I discourage that."

I said, "I see a problem here, Andrew. It looks like you'll be cast as a suspect."

"Looks like— No, wait!" He snapped his fingers. "Mrs. Gilmartin came by and called me through the window. I didn't even remember because she bends my ear every night, and I try to ignore her."

"What did she want?"

"I don't know, she was always— Oh, hold on, I remember now." He wagged his head in imitation. "She said she was glad Joey Buttafuoco was finally in jail. That's where he belonged, and she personally hoped they would throw away the key. His poor wife . . . " He waved his hand. " . . . Yada yada . . . "

Frank made no judgment about Buttafuoco. "Do you have Mrs. Gilmartin's address?"

"Not exactly. But if you'll come with me to the window . . . " He pushed aside the filmy curtain. "I can point to her house."

Mrs. Gilmartin was the neighborhood cat lady. She sat on her stoop, arrayed in the appropriate uniform of her calling, a limp polyester shirtwaist and unraveling cardigan. We had to wait while she dumped a can of Cozy Kitten on a paper plate for an impatient piebald tomcat and his juvenile apprentice.

"Now, Richard, be a good kitty and share with Howard."

She patted the tom, who genteelly took his repast from the south edge of the plate while his companion stuck his little white face in the north end.

"Yes, I always take my walk after Tom Brokaw, that's at six o'clock.

And I make conversation with Mr. Berry, just to show I'm a friendly person. *He's* not very friendly, but I just keep trying."

"What did you talk about the evening before last?"

"Oh, how would I remember? I talk to him every evening."

I prodded. "Wasn't that the day Joey Buttafuoco went to jail?"

"Oh, that day?" She lifted her head. "And it was about time too!" She shook her finger. "I just hope they threw away the key. I told Mr. Berry that."

When we had bid her leave and turned the corner, I said, "She's right. It *was* the day Buttafuoco went to jail."

"So Andrew's alibi looks pretty good for now."

"Yes."

"I was thinking that Richard must be gay."

"Huh? Richard who?"

"Richard the tomcat. Why else would he be so accommodating to that kitten, Howard?"

"Kittens aren't born knowing how to be cats; they have to be taught."

"So their mothers teach them to catch mice and so forth."

"Sometimes the mother is too busy, so a neighborhood male enlists in the 'Big Brother' program."

"That's great. I wish *people* would do that."

Julian heard the scraping as I parked the car and met me at the gate.

"Margo, you get the bad news first and there's no good news."

"Oh, nuts. Okay. Hit me."

"I found out David Ariane's station is flying a professor of Gaelic studies in from New York City for tomorrow night. And Randall Jooby has a friend coming in from Philadelphia who understands the language. Plus, there are whisperings of at least three other reporters who've got experts coming in."

"Gee. That's a whole bunch."

"Exactly! They'll be in every corner of the auditorium."

"You were wrong. It's *good* news. The more the merrier in this case."

Mavourneen, I'm having the worst trouble with my fourteen-year-old daughter, Tiffany."

I looked through my hands to see the first querent Andrew had recognized. A slender, well-dressed blond approaching middle age.

"Oh, goodness! Tell me about it."

"Well, she just defies me. She stays out till all hours, and I'm afraid she's experimenting with drugs!"

" 'Tis the fault o' her friends." I lifted two stitches onto my cable needle. I had almost finished the front of Julian's sweater.

"Yes," the woman crowed. "That's right!"

Easy guess there. The Devil's own mother would claim that he misbehaves only because of the bad example of the companions he's been hanging out with in hell.

I put two fingers to my brow. "Her grandmother has the answer."

"Really? You think I should send Tiffany to her grandmother in Ohio?"

"Aye, 'tis a much more wholesome place fer a girl."

"That's what I was thinking. Oh, thank you. I'm going to write to my mother tonight!"

"Mavourneen?" It was a muffin-faced girl who put her hand up, then stood and raised her voice self-consciously. "I was wondering . . . Who are you making the sweater for?"

"Oh, dearie me." (Gad! I wasn't expecting that one. I couldn't very well say it was for Julian Fortier, someone Mavourneen didn't even know. Think fast.)

"Why, darlin', Oim knittin' this ta donate ta the brave lads who are riskin' their loives ta foight fer a free Oireland!"

Then arose a young plaintive cry. "Mavourneen? My boyfriend, Curtis, and I are really in love—"

I shoved my hand out in a "stop" sign. "Don't do it, darlin'."

"How did you know what I was going to ask?"

"Make him stand up with ye bayfore ye loie down with him."

"What does that mean?"

"Get married first."

"Well, he can't marry me right now, but he shows that he loves me."

I was between rows, so shook my free needle.

"Thar's only one way fer a young man ta show he loves ye. That is, he'd be proud ta make ye his woife."

A clean-cut type who looked like a young Phil Collins raised his hand.

Andrew pointed with his chin. "Do you have a question for Mavourneen?"

"*Seadh,*" the man said. ("Yes.") "*Cé hé seipeal a cuaigh tú, nuair a bí tu az fás suas agus cé an aoiri a bí ann?*" ("Which church did you attend while you were growing up, and who was the pastor?")

"*An cuid is mo go ma saol, cuaiz me go dti Naom Malachy,*" I replied cheerfully. ("For most of my life, I went to St. Malachy's.") "*Bè an Tatair O'Floinn a bì ina aoire.*" ("And the pastor was Father O'Flynn.")

"*An raibh cabhroír aige?*" ("Did he have an assistant?")

"*An cagair O'Fanín, fear an deas a bí ann na blianta dearnac.*" ("Yes, and a very charming one in the latter years, Father Feenan.")

"*Go raibh maith agat.*" ("Thank you.")

"*Ta failte duit.*" ("You're welcome.")

There was dead silence for a moment, then someone boomed, "That's perfect Gaelic!" and whispered conferences were heard in spots around the auditorium.

Back in my dressing room, Frank was waiting and shaking his head. "I'll never understand that trick, Margo. I heard that one of those Gaelic experts threw a question at you and you were able to *answer* him!"

"It was easy." I laughed lightly. "After some twenty hours of rehearsal."

"You mean you rehearsed the answer? But how did you know what the question would be?"

Julian brought in my industrial-sized jar of cold cream.

"It was a setup, Frank."

I pulled my hair out of my face and clumped it together in an elastic. "Since every one of those cynics hauled in a Gaelic expert to test me, it didn't occur to any of them that I might have one of my *own*. That was my friend Patrick O'Flaherty. He's from Connemara, where they still speak the old language."

"O'Flaherty sings Irish ballads in a club down in the Quarter," Julian said. "He was kind enough to teach her that little exchange word by word."

"What was it about, by the way?"

"No big deal. Something about what church Mavourneen went to."

"Andrew had his orders." Julian looked around and lowered his voice. "He was to call on Patrick and then only on people he recognized, or African-Americans. There aren't too many black Gaelic professors."

"So that clears that up. But how did you know about Tiffany's grandmother?"

"Who?"

"Remember the girl who was running around in bad company?"

"Oh that. Well, a fourteen-year-old kid probably has at least one grandmother living."

"If she didn't?"

"Then I would have said that the *spirit* of Tiffany's grandmother was standing next to me, whispering in my ear."

"How did you guess that the girl should be shipped off to Ohio?"

"I didn't. All I needed to say was that her grandmother has the answer. Then the woman pretty much filled it in herself. The way she suggested Tiffany's going to live with her indicated that she'd already been thinking about it."

"But how did you know the grandmother lived in some wholesome place?"

"That woman said Ohio, for pity's sake. How boringly wholesome can you get? Also she was well dressed and well spoken, so obviously she hadn't come out of any slum tenement. And let's face it. A town doesn't have to be *too* idyllic to be a better climate for kids than New Orleans."

"Yes," Julian sighed. "We should have a sign at the city limits: ADULTS ONLY. And about that little piece of advice to the teenager about her rutting boyfriend, Curtis. You forget this is the 1990s, dear."

"No, but *you* forget that Mavourneen is living in the *eighteen*-nineties."

"Even so, do you think it's realistic to tell a girl to hold out for marriage?"

"Maybe not, but she should hold out for *something*." I dropped my bag on the table. "These girls don't realize what they're doing to themselves, giving it away for a few kind words."

"They don't think of consensual sex as giving anything away. This is supposed to be the age of equality."

"There's no such thing as sexual equality, Julian. Girls get a hundred-percent pregnant; boys get *zero* pregnant." I packed away my paint. "My own case is the best illustration. I'm forty-eight years old. I've said 'No' a lot of times, and I've said 'Yes' a lot of times."

"A lot more often, I'd venture."

"But the point is that now from the great light of hindsight, I don't regret any of the *no*s."

"But you regret some of the *yes*es?"

"I'll say. Especially the one to that vice cop in Chicago."

"Point made."

*W*hat's on the tube?"

Julian had his usual death grip on the remote.

"ESPN. Larry Holmes is fighting in Vegas."

"Wasn't he from a long time ago?"

"Right." Julian muted the volume. "Before Holyfield, before Tyson, before Michael Spinks."

"I'd thought Holmes was happily settled into life as a rich business-man in Easton, Pennsylvania."

"That's true. But it seems he wanted some new venture capital, so de-cided to get back in shape and revive his career."

"You think the guy's still got the fighting spirit after living as a mil-lionaire executive these past ten years?"

"He says he does."

"That may be worth seeing." I took a chair. "Look. What a pretty round card girl."

"That's his opponent."

I got up again.

"I have to finish my column."

I turned on the computer, ruminated over the blank space on the screen for a while, then typed in a little filler item:

"Local astrologer Howie Potts predicts a humongous earthquake to occur right after 'the big conjunction in Capricorn' on January 11. He can't tell us where, but says it will exact a great cost. We'll be watching the newscasts, Howie!"

When the phone rang, I clicked on "File" and "Save" before picking it up.

"Thrill me."

"Miss Fortier? This is Dan Aparisi."

"Oh, hi . . . I—"

He broke in on my fumbled greeting. "Listen. I don't know if this means anything or not, but it's about that actress Delphine hired."

"To play Miss Rosen's mother. Yes?"

"Well, I was visiting my grandma today, and I saw that same actress on one of her stories."

"A soap opera?"

"Yes, *Guiding Light*. Grandma said she's a semiregular character called Lucinda. And she's been coming on for maybe six months."

I thanked him, then hung up and pressed number three on my speed dial. It was picked up on the second ring.

"Martin, I don't know if this means anything, but the actress hired to scam your aunt has been appearing on *Guiding Light*."

"*Guiding Light?*" He seemed to hold his breath for a long moment. "Aunt Harriet never missed that program."

"I feel that I'm about to put my hand on the murderer." Frank shook his pen and made a note. "Here's how Dan Aparisi helped us reconstruct the scenario."

I flicked on my recorder. "Let's have it."

"The old woman Delphine swindled, Harriet Rosen, was a believer, but she wasn't senile. She wasn't stupid, either. Her sole frivolous indulgence was following the soap operas on TV." Frank shrugged tiredly. "One afternoon, she was watching *Guiding Light* and recognized an actress in a bit part. The name was different and the dress, but the face and voice were unmistakable."

I nodded. "It was the actress who played her mother in the phony séances."

"The same. We surmise that Miss Rosen didn't write to her nephew about her discovery, but determined to confront Delphine's gang of thieves herself. Her chauffeur confirmed that he drove her up to Delphine's the day before she died and that Delphine had been alone in the house. The old woman must have gone there to demand her money back. That was her fatal mistake."

I made sure the cassette reels were turning. "You surmise?"

"Reconstructing events, Delphine could have calmed her down, promised to make restitution or anything else she could think of to buy some time." Frank held out a medical examiner's report form. "Then she gave her a present. We don't know whether it was candy or cookies, but it must have been something sweet to cover the taste. It contained a heavy dose of arsenic."

"You know that only because Martin had her exhumed yesterday."

"Which I give him credit for. Immediately after seeing the old woman, Delphine caught a plane to Chicago and stayed there till she heard the 'all clear' sign the next day. Miss Rosen's maid came in to work and found her dead in her bed."

I tapped the report form. "No one suspected murder. When an eighty-year-old woman dies, they bury her. Period."

"So Delphine killed Miss Rosen, then Hubie Nadler was hired to kill her in retaliation." Frank held his hands out. "Who had both the motive and the money to pay a hitman? Your boyfriend, Martin Koenig."

"You don't mean to arrest *him*?"

"I'll admit we need more evidence. But he looks good for it."

3 5

"The bullet that killed Queen Marie came out of Hubie Nadler's rifle." I was at my word processor, talking while typing. "That's for sure."

Julian didn't look up from his paper. "So the killer of phony psychics has been brought to his own kind of justice."

"And the update on Nadler is finished, with my byline." I hit the return key. "Now I'll be happy to drop the Mavourneen act." I clicked on "File" and then again on "Print" and sat back to wait for the hard copy. "I'll have to thank Andrew. He was a great stage manager."

"Hmmpf." Julian turned a page. "I hope he was good with lights and sets. The man doesn't know beans about dramatization."

"Why do you say that?"

"Remember how he raved on and on about studying all the great playwrights: Williams, Ibsen, Shaw—"

"So what?"

"Not even a mention of the greatest of all. Right?"

"You're right. And I thought he was just about to say it too. Shakespeare. But"—I replayed the conversation in my head—"he came out with James Shirley instead." Then came the dawn "Julian!" I pounded the table. "He *had* to!"

"What?"

I dialed his number, and he answered with a bored, "Yeah?"

"Andrew? The police believe the hitman, Nadler, was hired to kill Delphine."

"That makes sense to me," he admitted. "But who would have hired him?"

"Frank thinks it was Martin Koenig."

"No." There was a slight pause, then, "I know Koenig, and I don't believe it."

"Me neither. And I think you can help me prove it was Dr. Ingram!"

"Ingram?"

"Meet me at that vacant building at the corner of Burgundy and Montegut. Two hours."

"Right."

I let Andrew into the building, and he wrinkled his nose at the dust.

"This place hasn't been occupied in three years," I said by way of apology, and turned on the naked bulb overhead.

Andrew followed me into the room, strewn with a few sticks of old, not antique, furniture.

"It's isolated enough."

"I didn't want to be overheard. Because what I did wasn't exactly legal."

His ears pricked up at that. "No?"

I turned back to the door, locked it, and put the key in my purse. "Now we know we're alone."

He glanced around the nearly empty room, then started toward a huge console TV of stained and chipped blond wood near the front wall.

"Maybe it works," I said. "Why don't you plug it in while we're talking? Sally Jessy is interviewing women who are dealing with life after hysterectomies."

Andrew drew back in disgust. "Forget it."

No man wants to watch Sally Jessy.

He took a seat on a red plastic milk carton. "You said you have something to implicate Ingram?"

"It's a copy of a check Ingram made out to Delphine. But I got it by extralegal means." I winked as I handed it over. "And there was something else we have to discuss."

He read the photocopy and folded it. "What?"

"Shakespeare."

He shifted slightly. "How's that?"

"You bragged about all the great playwrights whose work you've performed. But you didn't mention the greatest of them all, Shakespeare."

"So what?"

"The omission was rather glaring, and we wondered why. Till we realized you couldn't call attention to the fact that, like any classically trained actor, you had to have studied *fencing*."

"Sure." He shrugged. "Four semesters at the academy. That hardly makes me Cyrano de Bergerac."

"Don't be so modest. Frank just got a copy of the transcript; you pulled straight As in that course. So you had the talent and the opportunity. The only element still missing was the motive. That was, until I went back to Harriet Rosen. I finally realized it wasn't Delphine Miss Rosen confronted about the fraud, but you."

"I had to do all the dirty work in the organization," he sneered. "I put my oblivious partner on a plane to Chicago, then drove over to the old bat's house with a box of cookies. Eventually, Frieda figured out how I'd handled the matter. But then instead of being grateful, she threatened to lead the cops right to my door unless I signed my percentage of the business over to her." He made two fists. "I remember how she just stood there and smiled triumphantly, as though she'd come up with something very clever. At that minute, picking up the saber and running her through was the most natural action in the world."

"And you didn't put Sidney onstage because he could imitate Bette Davis. He must have been blackmailing you."

"Frieda had told him everything about how we met, and he doped out the significance of the Pluto glyph."

"So you pretended to make him your partner and let him play swami."

"I had to jolly him along. But it was a risk. God! One more swishy female impersonation act like that and we'd have been out of business permanently."

"As a matter of curiosity, why did you let *me* on with my Irish impersonation act?"

"Only to get you out of the way. When you started yammering about checking into Frieda's past, her schools, her jobs, I knew I couldn't let that happen. First I sent Hubie Nadler to take care of the problem, but he blew it."

"That's a shame. He left me alive to look for some connection between Nadler and whoever hired him. I finally realized you were the only one in the case who had anything in common with Nadler. You were both experts in character makeup."

"Is that so?" Andrew nonchalantly moved between me and the front door.

"He was known as a master of disguise." I raised a finger. "And you said you got great reviews for your portrayal of Lincoln. That would have involved great skill with makeup."

He nodded. "It did."

"I'd bet it was you who made the actress up to look like Harriet Rosen's mother."

"It was," he conceded. "Hubie and I met at a theatrical supply store three years ago."

"Let me guess. It was Duchess Theatrical Supplies, right?"

"How did you know?"

"Because the proprietor had seen you two together. That was why Nadler tried to kill him."

"Yeah, so he wouldn't tell anyone about the connection. Just a precaution. Nothing personal against the old man." He put one hand in his jacket pocket, and I heard something click. "When I first knew Hubie, he was doing these false beards that looked absolutely ridiculous. I taught him how to make beards and mustaches that were fairly undetectable even in sunlight, then onto false teeth, prosthetics, the whole catalog."

"In gratitude for your tutelage, he volunteered to take me out?"

"Not entirely. I offered to pay his usual fee. He really screwed it up, though, and just made the whole situation messier. Hubie made himself useful one last time, croaking that voodoo broad. But then when you and the lieutenant started throwing his name around, I knew his time was up. He couldn't be taken alive."

"So as a practical matter, you framed him for Delphine. By the way, how did you manage to shoot him with his own gun?"

"I went to his hotel room with a present, a brand new .357 Magnum. I made a big show of putting bullets in for him, but there was no powder in the shells. He was impressed enough to lay his own weapon down."

"While he was enjoying the Magnum, you killed him, then put Delphine's ring in his pocket."

"I thought that would close the case. But you! . . ." He bared his teeth. "You! . . . You weren't satisfied with that."

"Nadler had no connection with Delphine and home-invasion wasn't his M.O. . . . Where was the motive?"

"So I had to resort to a distraction, the same that worked with Sidney. I figured you were stagestruck and the more time you spent rehearsing that asinine brogue, the less you had to research the case."

"So . . . uh . . . " I raised my voice in hurt and outrage. "It didn't have anything to do with how *good* I was as Mavourneen?!"

"Hell, no! I thought you'd finally get bored with the whole subject and go flitting back to your society trivia. Then maybe I could put together a deal with Irma Thomas."

"I didn't appreciate your trick with my gas jet, either."

He turned his lips up like a smile. "It was a fifty-to-one shot, but I didn't have anything to lose by trying."

"In that case, I will be happy to see you sent away for murder."

"You?" He shook his head in profound disbelief. "You are one hell of a stupid cunt." He took his hand out of his pocket, and I saw the glint of the knife blade. "You really thought I would let you walk out of here?"

"Uh . . . Yes."

"I think so too!" Marilou Gendron's voice crackled behind him. "Put your knife down slowly!"

Andrew reeled around, to see the officer in a two-handed firing stance with the Police Special pointed at his left ventricle, decided she basically wasn't kidding, and did as she said.

"Now point it to your right and lay it on the floor, carefully, and take two steps forward."

208

He obeyed in total bewilderment.

"But the room was *empty*! Where the hell were you?"

"In the television." Marilou jerked her thumb over her shoulder.

"That's all illusion and misdirection," I crowed. "What was formerly a common household television was gutted and transformed into a temporary police station. Custom-built for one particular officer."

Marilou walked behind Andrew and put one foot on his back as she cuffed his hands behind him.

"Ask Lieutenant Washington to join us."

I sat on the bumper of Frank's unit, with a cruller in one hand and a pen in the other. My pad was on my lap.

"So now Andrew Berry is going to be surrounded by iron for the rest of his life, wouldn't you say? Iron bars, iron doors, iron walls . . ."

"That's a fair guess," Frank agreed. "So what's your point?"

"Well, he should have known better than to threaten that priest, Guillermo. He was messing with Oggūn, the god of *iron*."

"The gods work in mysterious ways. Your friend Andrew decided to make the Pluto sign his own trademark, to obscure the fact that it was a dying message giving away his identity."

I took a bite of my cruller for sustenance. "After he killed Sidney, he had to direct us away from Delphine and her organization. They were supposed to appear as just two victims in a series. The other murder was a smoke screen."

"It's clear now that Queen Marie was chosen because she had no connection to Andrew. Then he made a threat against that Afro-Cuban priest to take us even farther afield."

"He figured that with half the squad occupied in guarding Sanchez, there would be no one following through on the primary victim."

"I didn't suspect Andrew in Nadler's death, because he had an alibi," Frank admitted.

"Not a real one."

"Old Mrs. Doohickey with the cats said he spoke to her."

"No, Frank. If you analyze her statement, she actually said *she* spoke to *him*. She didn't take note that there was no reply, because she's used to being ignored."

"But she saw him up there."

"Through a filmy curtain. Instructions on how to make a realistic latex face mask is theatrical makeup one-oh-one. All he had to do was tack it onto a wig stand and prop the whole thing up by the window."

"It couldn't have been a wig stand; she saw him moving."

"How much mechanical ability does it take to make an armature that would move a rocking chair on the same principle as a metronome? He used gadgets like that in his phony séances."

"But how could he have recalled the conversation?"

"The answer to that is so simple, you'll kick yourself. Andrew simply turned on a tape recorder before he left the house. Then when he came home, he just played back everything he would have heard if he had actually been sitting in that rocker all the time. Do you have any more background for my feature?"

"Just one item," Frank said too casually. "We finally got Berry's employment records from California. He and Frieda Harris had worked together in a theme park, all right. That part was true. But it wasn't Knott's Berry Farm as he claimed; it was *Disneyland*." He raised his eyebrows. "And it turns out that Frieda didn't play a dance hall girl after all. She played Snow White."

"You don't say."

"Really. And Andrew wasn't a cowboy, either." Now Frank grinned a Cheshire-cat grin. "Can you guess which particular cartoon character he dressed up as?"

"I don't want to hear it."

36

*T*he close and curious were crowded up against the gate, and I counted four video cameras. I had to remind myself not to smile for them.

"Ladies and gentlemen! . . ."

Then I noticed David Ariane, who must have been ordered to come. He tried to make himself inconspicuous behind a clump of print newsies but was too tall to manage it. I was mean enough to issue him a cheery wave.

"Ladies and gentlemen," I said again. "I have called you here to make an announcement about Mavourneen Rose Kerrigan."

"You have traced her down?" someone called excitedly.

"Yes, I have! And there really was such a person." I gave a dramatic pause. "But there was nothing at all paranormal about my recollections of her."

"No!" several women protested. And one called, "What was it then?"

"I have been advised that what I thought was a channeled entity must have been nothing more than a phenomenon of my own hidden memory."

There were some murmurs and two or three gasps of surprise. But the prevailing reaction among newshounds was the characteristic shrug of "I knew it all along."

A pencil was raised like a flag. "Mrs. Fortier? Why didn't you tell us this before."

"Because I just got the answer last night." I took the photograph out of my bag and held it to the WDSU camera. "This is my great-grandmother, Mavourneen Kerrigan Armaugh. She died when I was only four."

The visual aid caught their attention, and cameramen shouldered one another aside vying for the best angle.

"Mrs. Fortier?" a blond field reporter shrilled. "Do you mean to say you were pretending to be her?"

"Oh, no!" (Fat chance I'd admit to *that*.) "It was all subconscious. Granny used to take care of me, and I loved her so much I just—"

"Internalized her personality!" called a man in the rear of the crowd. "And it just reemerged briefly. It's called *Gabrielle's Syndrome*."

"Thank you, I—" At that moment, Julian galloped out to join me, bumped into my elbow, and the photo dropped to the cement step, breaking the glass.

"Oh, what'd I do?! Sorry." He stepped to the microphone. "Ladies and gentlemen of the press. I've just had a call from the D.A.'s office. Andrew Berry has been formally arraigned on four charges of murder."

Pencils moved frantically, *scratch scratch scratch,* while cameramen took their video recorders off their shoulders and packed them up. The story about me was over.

Only David Ariane still held his microphone aloft. "Tell us something about *Gabrielle's Syndrome!*"

"What?" I was hunkered down, picking up shards of glass. "I never heard of it before."

A WWL reporter turned around. "Where's that guy who was talking about it? I want to interview *him*. Where'd he go?"

"I dunno," his cameraman said.

"But . . ." A tired-looking woman in her fifties waved her hand. "We came to see *Mavourneen*. What about our questions?"

I stood upright just as the microphone stand was being dismantled.

"We don't have anyone to give us the answers anymore. It looks like we have to find them for ourselves. In here." I tapped my chest. "But then . . . maybe they were here all along."

The event was over, and our disillusioned audience withdrew, trudging off in clumps.

Julian locked the door after us and hooked the chain.

"That was handled very nicely, dear. Misdirection to the end."

I kicked my shoes off and flopped on the couch.

"Brad did a great job, piping up with an explanation about a syndrome that never existed. And being a romantic, he named it after his girlfriend, Gaby."

"Do give some credit for *my* little charade. Knocking your picture down gave Brad a chance to make his escape and, at the same time, bring symbolic closure to the whole episode."

"By the time anyone realizes there's no such thing as *Gabrielle's Syndrome,* I'll be stale old news." Then I remembered something and felt around my bra. "It's gone."

"Your figure? I could have told you."

"No, I mean the little charm Guillermo made to protect me from evil."

"So, it's done its job and gone on to better things. By the way, when are you going to knit me another sweater?"

"Maybe next incarnation."

"Sure. You might come back as somebody who actually *cares* about a person."

"That would be a treat— Oh, there goes the phone." I stretched my legs out and wiggled my toes. "If only I were four years younger, I'd jump right up and answer it."

"I get the hint." Julian (who *is* four years younger) sprinted to the telephone, said "Hi ho!" into it, then held the receiver against his chest and beckoned. "It's your brother."

"Yippie!" I heaved off the couch and nearly kicked over the table in my haste to grab the phone, snatched the receiver, and fell backward *(thunk)* into the nearest chair. "Hey, Tommy!"

"Sis! I just got in from Bermuda and heard your frantic messages. What is it you need?"

"Never mind. Last week, I wanted some advice, but everything's cool now."

"Uh-oh. What have you been up to?"

"Listen, it's great. I was on the stage!"

"Not stripping again, Margie! You didn't look *that* good twenty years ago, and I don't see—"

"Rest assured, I worked fully dressed this time. I was posing as a psychic channeler to get a story. You should have seen it."

"A channeler?" He laughed dryly. "How the dickens did you pull that off, Sis?"

"It wasn't so tough. All I had to do was put on this neat brogue, you know, like our great-grandma's? And then I just repeated the stories she used to tell me."

I detected a sharp intake of breath on the other end.

"You don't mean Granny Armaugh!"

"Sure. I know you couldn't remember her, Tommy. She died in 1950, before you were born."

"But Aunt Loretta told me she went through her surgery in 1943. That was before *you* were born."

"Right. They used to talk about it. Some kind of cancer, as I recall."

There was a full ten seconds of silence before Tom spoke again.

"It was her *larynx,* Margie. They had to take it out."

"Her larynx?" My knuckles grew white on the receiver. "What are you saying?"

"Only that during the last seven years of her life, Granny Armaugh could not have uttered *one word*."